JACARANDA JOURNAL

Jacaranda Journal, Volume 11, Edition 1, Exposed Roots is published by Jacaranda Journal with the ongoing support of The University of Queensland School of Communication and Arts and Faculty of Humanities, Arts and Social Sciences.
jacarandajournaluq@gmail.com
jacarandajournaluq.com.au

Cover and typesetting by Siena Johnstone and Francis Harvey
Cover photograph by Torrey Atkin
Printed by IngramSpark

This edition would not be possible without the sponsoprship of Synergy Management and Tendered, and the support of The University of Queensland.

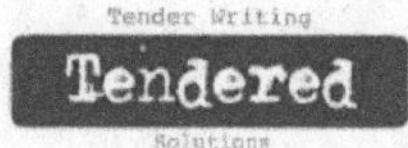

JACARANDA JOURNAL

Edition 11.1
Exposed Roots

Jacaranda Journal acknowledges the Turrbul and Yuggera peoples as Traditional Owners and Custodians of the lands on which The University of Queensland operates. We pay our respects to their ancestors and their descendants, who continue cultural and spiritual connections to country. We recognise their valuable contributions to Australian and global society.

We are indebted to Australia's First Nations peoples who have shared their stories on Country for more than 65,000 years.

Editorial Team

Jacaranda is made up of a supportive and ambitious community of emerging editors who champion local voices and emerging writers. We thank them all for their generous contributions to this edition.

Contents

NON-FICTION

Letter from the Editors

FRANCIS HARVEY & SIENA JOHNSTONE

It may surprise you to read that Jacarandas are an introduced species. It certainly surprised us. Hailing from the subtropics of South America, the first recorded Australian Jacaranda was planted in Brisbane in 1864. Due to familiar climatic conditions, and the popularity of the tree's purple flowers, Jacarandas quickly took root throughout the area. In the intervening 160 years, they have grown to become a charismatic part of Brisbane's cityscape.

Every spring, purple canopies bloom across the river city's broad streets, and across many small southeast Queensland towns besides. Thousands of locals and tourists turn out to admire the spectacle—Brisbane's very own, garish, daggy cherry blossom. The University of Queensland's Saint Lucia campus contains an especially impressive stand of the trees, and it was after these that Jacaranda Journal was originally named, over a decade ago now.

But if you were surprised to discover Jacarandas were introduced, you'll be even more surprised to discover Brisbane City Council lists them as an invasive species. Turns out Jacaranda's have hardy, fast growing root systems, which gives them the problematic ability to outcompete local flora. Take a look at a Jacaranda next time you pass one, and you'll probably see a bare patch surrounding its base.

The tree's listing as an invasive species is a difficult thing to square with its beloved status in Brisbane culture. Jacarandas embody a tangled relationship that requires some genuine intellectual creativity to unpick, and the unpicking reveals some challenging questions. Is it possible for an invasive species to belong? Could it be, that the Jacaranda's fraught relationship with origin and ecosystem is what makes it such a relatable symbol? Or is it just something about those pretty purple flowers?

It is these questions, and many more besides, that we've encouraged our contributors to contemplate in this first ever themed edition of Jacaranda: Exposed Roots. We put the call out for works that respond to questions of belonging, of growth and change, of ecology and origin, and we've been blown away by the responses we've received.

From poetic meditations on interconnectedness, to creative non-fiction exploring evolving cityscapes, to short fiction that narrates the challenging adaptations undertaken by immigrant communities, each contribution resonates with our prompt in its own surprising and unique way.

We'd like to take this opportunity to thank our phenomenal contributors. It has been a privilege to share this creative journey with you. Your work has entertained us and inspired us, challenging us to see, listen and learn in new and profound ways. We are honoured to showcase your work.

Thank you also to our editorial team for your tireless efforts. As editors of this edition, our shared mission has been to offer our contributors the support and space needed to nurture their work to its full potential. Each member of our team has brought deep tenderness and care to the delicate process of editing, and we are proud to call each of you a member of Jacaranda Journal.

Finally, to our supporters, our sponsors, and our community, thank you. This edition has been brought to life for you.

Your Editors in Chief
Francis Harvey & Siena Johnstone

Moulded Pear

JAEDYN LIEBENBERG

Home is where the mould is.

Sumito first noticed this on a sunny Wednesday afternoon, sat underneath his Mother's favourite Keyaki tree. An ant crawled across his book page. He swatted it away. Another would come back shortly.

The soil beneath Sumito was rich. It twisted between the fibres of his pants and embedded them with a sour, earthy scent. Bark wedged between his left shoulder blade and spine. The rigid strip prodded through his loose shirt and pinched at a nerve. Sumito tightened his jaw in discomfort.

He shifted his weight to the right. He reread the last line of his book. Still, the pain lingered.

Beyond his bend of shade, Sumito's Mother stood in the wheat fields at the edge of their farm. She wore old clothes, patched and resewn with offcuts and thread from the local market. Her skirt drifted in the wind as she harvested seedheads. Sumito watched her. She was angry.

She tore moulded seedheads out whole—ripped them from their rows, and let the soil erupt. The rotten stems would be carried home and burnt beneath their fireplace wood. Golden rows swelled around her when the wind gusted again. Wheat enveloped her distant figure as she continued through. She moved further inwards, away from the dirt road and tyre tracks from four days prior.

When Sumito slipped a bookmark between two pages, he recalled his Father would be home tonight. He stared at his Mother for a moment longer.

Her straw hat and dark hair wafted violently. He wondered, as the roots he sat against protruded into his lower back, whether her emotions could seep into the soil she touched. And, if she tried hard enough, would the ground truly bend to her anger as Sumito felt it already did? The crops might wilt if she could. Then, what would she do in the hours she ignored him?

Novel underneath his arm, Sumito left the tree to return home.

"You don't need to help with dinner."

Sumito looked up from the carrots he had been cutting. He dug his nails into his palm.

"Well, I would like to." He continued to cut. The knife jutted against the wooden board, a sharp chop and scrape to move each slice.

His Mother's stare bore into him. *Chop*. Her eyes flickered down to the vegetable. *Chop*. She looked back to Sumito. *Chop*. Her lips scrunched together in a frown.

"Your Father might not want carrots."

"He's not home yet," Sumito said, voice unwavering. "He can pick them out if he doesn't want them."

"Do you really think after four days of working, and five hours of driving, he'll want to pick out carrots? Don't be stupid. Throw them out."

"No."

"Excuse me?"

Sumito placed down the knife.

"I can't believe you," his Mother began. "You haven't spoken to me for three days and the first thing you want to do is argue?"

Sumito straightened his back. The joints along his neck clicked. His dry swallow resounded through his ears.

His Mother's skin swelled with the roots that hid underneath. They spread her wrinkles out until the flesh ran taut. Her undereye dotted with black, like fruit forgotten on the bottom fridge shelf, and spilled the rot of her three days silence.

The rot permeated Sumito. He was her product—her blossom of all she harboured. And he could *feel* that. The splinters that drove through her skin may as well have been from his hand. She was decaying. At his expense. His fault.

"Are you just going to stare?" His Mother scoffed.

Sumito met his Mother's eyeline. She held her usual scorn and nothing more.

The screen door hinges squeaked open.

His Mother's expression dissipated into a pleasant neutral.

"Honey," she spoke, heading for the door.

Mumbles of "welcome home" and "how was the trip?" came down the hall. Sumito knew he was meant to go and greet his Father as well.

He reached for another carrot and began to cut again.

While his Mother grabbed his Father's coat, and briefcase, and bags, he limited his acknowledgements to "hm" and "good". His suit was old. He bought it the week Sumito turned two. Over the years it had fit him well, and then not at all. Presently, it ran loose around his legs, but tightened to near tears over his stomach.

"Have you eaten yet, honey?" his Mother's voice echoed down as the screen door screeched shut.

"Not yet."

"Well dinner is still a bit away. Did you want some tea, or I'll cut some fruit, or—"

"Nice to see you too." His Father stood at the kitchen doorframe, staring down Sumito.

Sumito pressed his lips upwards in the shadow of a smile. Without looking up, he could imagine the distant expression his Father held. His glasses frame would press further down his nose when his eyebrows furrowed together. The lines on his forehead would remain as he waited for a response. Only the tip of his tongue would tut against his teeth when he did not get one.

"You have a letter." His Father grabbed an envelope from his back pocket. "Keio University."

The knife miscut the carrot. It slanted on the back half.

"Never heard of them."

His Father placed the envelope on the countertop. Sumito glanced at the familiar emblem stamped onto the corner. He did not say a word. Nor did his Father.

Sumito tightened his grasp on the knife as it miscut another chop. He did not look back at the envelope. From the corner of his eye, his parents loomed, waiting.

Cheap metal frames dug into his Father's nose and upper cheek. They pressed further into his flesh until roots rose from the wound. Poisoned leaves and moulded stems pooled just as tears would. They spilt down to connect at his Father's chin. As they ran, they tore through his cheeks like a dormant illness, now desperate to spread.

Sumito knew it spread unto him. The strength that held the knife steady between his fingers was prickled with thorns. They buried into his skin, familiar and fatherly. He could not be better. He did not know what qualified *better*.

Standing beside his Father, Sumito's Mother corroded like diseased wheat. The roots below her skin coiled around her neck. Choked her. Forced her tan skin to mar into a crisp charcoal. Betrayal poured from the cracks between her dry knuckles. Her fingers reached out—resistantly, as if Sumito was holding her beneath soil until she went limp.

She grasped onto Sumito's shoulder. "We agreed on the university twenty minutes down, didn't we, Sumito?"

He stopped.

"I said I wanted to look at other options as well." He could not look at her. "Tsurui is a small town. I could do better elsewhere, closer to—"

"Tokyo."

"—Tokyo," Sumito finished, meeting his Mother's eyes. She wore her frown like a treetop unwillingly bent back into the ground, dragging down past her neck.

Sumito shifted his eyes. Her frown appeared more impartial at once.

"Do you think of anyone but yourself?"

Sumito's throat tightened around a reply he would not say.

"No, you don't. And you know that." His Mother wiped away tears. "You do this on purpose. Again, and again."

"Did you think I was going to live here the rest of my life?" Sumito choked around the question, wanting to swallow it back down the moment he dared to speak.

His Mother wept.

"Sumito," his Father scolded. "No one was saying that. But you need to realise how what you say makes people feel."

Sumito was too accustomed to their words to feign hurt.

"I know that. But when I'm trying to tell you what I want with my—"

"What you want? Sumito, it is *always* what you want," his Mother spoke into her handkerchief. "Your Father and I have given up so much for you, yet you want this, and you *want* that. You have no consideration for what either of us wants."

"What you want me to do with *my* life?"

"Yes. Do we not get any input as your parents?"

"Yes, but—"

"So why do you do this? Do you enjoy upsetting us both? Ruining dinner? Stressing out your Father when he's just gotten home, oh I—," his Mother sobbed. She stepped out of the room, leaving through the broken screen door that went into the yard.

Shifting his gaze, Sumito stood with his mouth hung ajar.

"I'm not trying to upset anyone," Sumito spoke to his mostly disinterested Father. 'I just want more than what life would be if I stayed here.'

"I understand that."

Sumito was taken aback.

"But..."

Ah.

"Your Mother was right. You should think of people other than just yourself, even if it is your life. Do you think I would do all this if I lived for only myself?"

Sumito would be foolish to answer his question. The answer kneaded into the bread Sumito's Mother made for his weeks away. It poured into the liquor bottles Sumito memorised before he could walk. He stared at his Father, wanting to feel his chest ache in disappointment.

But nothing came.

"I'll go look for your Mother," his Father said as he grabbed a pear from the fruit basket and bit into it. His expression soured. As he turned the fruit, it mushed under his fingertips.

His Father tossed the rotten fruit back onto the counter.

"And throw these away."

Sumito stared at the perfect edge of the pear that blended into a darkened sludge. The roots deep within his veins bulged.

How would it be to cut out the mould? Would he bleed from the loss as he extracted each root? Or would he grow back together? Perhaps, even if he carved himself out until he was hollow, the existence of his Mother and Father would remain.

Sumito picked up the pear.

He bit into the mould, savouring the damned curl in his throat.

Jaedyn is a literary fiction writer currently completing their Bachelor of Arts at UQ. When they are not questioning which genre their work fits into, they enjoy panic rewriting drafts and looping old albums for the hundredth time.

Origins

AMANDA WONG

Everything is wrong here.

Five years later and I'm still not used to the unnatural feeling whenever I step outside the house—the thrum of cicadas, the sweltering heat and still air. I squint up at the sky, wrapping my fingers tightly over the cool, familiar grooves of the rock in my pocket. My heart aches for grey skies, cracked pavement and the flickering wink of skyscrapers at night.

I'm almost knocked aside as my son barrels through the doorway into the front yard, skinny arms outstretched for balance. Something in my chest loosens slightly, seeing him run on the yellowed grass, sunlight glinting off his black hair.

"G'day, Aileen," a neighbour from across the street calls as he drags his bin down his driveway.

Ai Lian, the voice in my head corrects him. Outwardly, I nod back to him, my fingers again finding the smooth stone in my pocket. I inch my way towards the car parked on the side of the road.

"I see young Daniel there is enjoying himself," he says. "How old is he now?"

I hate that it takes me a second to find the right words. "He just turned six."

"Ah, so he'll be starting school then?"

"He's going today," I reply, haltingly. I hold onto the pebble like a prayer. Today my son will go down a different path, one where I can't protect him. He doesn't deserve to be treated poorly because we look different. It would break my heart if he came back one day resenting his heritage—resenting who we are.

"Ma, look at this!" Daniel calls out, waving a fist as he runs towards me. I manage to catch him in my arms just as his body slams into mine, and together we fall back onto the dry grass. His excited little puffs of air brush against my cheek as he holds his hand out. Despite myself, I lean forward.

A small spider scuttles quickly across his palm. I let out a strangled cry, my rock dropping from my fingertips. The neighbour chuckles as he ambles back up his driveway.

"Aiyah! What did I tell you about animals here?" I scold Daniel, clutching a hand to my chest, the other smacking his arm half-heartedly. He laughs merrily and I resist the urge to shake some sense into him.

"Ah-Ma, it wasn't dangerous, I know which ones to look out for," he declares.

"Get in the car before something bites you—we can't be late."

Through the rear-view mirror I can see Daniel as he chatters and gestures animatedly. My throat tightens as the car approaches the entrance. Fair-haired children stream toward the school doors, their shoulders relaxed with a luxury we could never afford. When we stand outside the car, I wrap my arms tightly around my son. I pull back, and he gives me a beaming smile.

"Come on," he says, tugging my hand. "Let's go meet my teacher."

I hesitate, my other hand fiddling with the stone. An immediate sense of unsettlement floods through my body until my gaze fixes upon the eucalyptus trees waving in the distance. They beckon me to explore this country, to learn it intimately with my son. For the first time, I feel new roots taking hold, connecting me to the place where I will raise him.

"One second," I tell him.

I carefully place the pebble into a nearby garden bed and squeeze Daniel's hand as I get back up. Together, we walk through the door.

Amanda is currently pursuing a dual degree at The University of Queensland specialising in music and writing. When she isn't tooting away on the flute, Amanda loves to read and write all kinds of storytelling. She is particularly interested in recapturing the ravenous reading experience people often had growing up.

Past Lives

LARA KENNY

The place we grew up, the place that made us, was a cluster of cramped, wooden houses pitched side by side along cracked bitumen roads. In the summer, the air throbbed impatiently, storm clouds rolling across the horizon only to melt out into pitter-patters on rusted roofs, dribbling warm and murky into our outstretched palms. This was all we ever knew, but the adults remembered days so cold that their lips cracked and numbed, and their feet swelled black and blue. Childhoods spent scraping ice out of gutters and sneaking snow down their siblings' shirts. Now, they had sunburnt foreheads and browned backs and carried screaming tools instead of snow in their man-sized hands.

It was 1952 and our families had been in Australia for five and a half years. Before that, we lived in a refugee camp in Germany. My memories from that time are fleeting moments that cleave through my vision unexpectedly. The boy with the cheeks that had been scooped out of his face, so that he looked more like an outline of a boy than a boy. The only other girl my age had eyes like two glassy marbles protruding from her skull. When she asked if she could play with me, I kicked awkwardly at the dirt, frightened of this strange, sad creature who looked like an old doll splitting at the seams.

You lived next door to me on the immigrant side of town. The part of town that smelt of pierogi, golabki, and kotlet schabowy. Of a home neither of us could remember. Our friendship was forged through sideway glances over the chain-link fence dividing our backyards, timid smiles exchanged while lying starfish style on the prickly lawn, to escape our mothers' temper. Years of mopping rich people's house made them tired and aching, quick to bite.

At eight, our fingertips were a mess of warts and splinters from hours spent clambering up tree branches and squeezing into the impossible spaces in the drain across the street. We liked to play in the creek bed down the road. The embankment was littered with mushy, half-eaten sandwiches and soggy shoes. When it rained, the stench rose up and bit our nostrils. The Australian children who lived on the high side of town—whose small mouths were already filled up with more English than anyone we knew—never came here. But to us, that quiet, filthy creek was the whole ocean. Every weekend, we played mermaids in the creek until our skin turned red and itchy with mosquito bites and we had to steal my mum's butter knife to claw dirt from beneath our chapped fingernails.

Our parents sent us to the same primary school, an arrangement of wooden demountables that groaned underfoot, a basketball court with faded yellow lines and weeds poking through the cracks slicing through the concrete. We sat side by side in the back row, away from the girls who carried books filled with words our tongues couldn't straddle, the sentences melting on our inexperienced lips. Away from our steely-eyed teacher and the metal ruler quivering in her restless palms, waiting for us to mumble no, sorry, I don't understand.

I always knew your father didn't like me. I remember his wide, stony figure straining against the seams of his fluorescent uniform. On Sundays, you would sit triumphant on his shoulders, your child-hands dancing along his cropped black hair as he trudged to the wooden Church two blocks away. The size of it couldn't hold a God. He wasn't even Catholic, you told me one day.

"But everybody here is," you explained.

Your father was willing to pray to a God he didn't believe in, kneel on hard wooden pews until his knees crackled and popped, just to avoid being different. So that when he spoke to someone at the grocery store, they wouldn't care about the way his accent made his words tumble together like a building with crooked foundations. He went to church because he wanted to be normal. Because what is a prayer if not a plea for sameness? Because church is the place where your voice stops being your voice, sucked into the hum of one hundred people all saying the same words, making the same sounds.

On Sunday mornings I visited the lolly shop across the street from the church and snuck freckles and freddo frogs into the frayed pockets of my overalls. Once, your father caught my eye as I scuttled out onto the footpath and shoved an entire chocolate bar between my teeth, the way I'd seen my brother do it. He glared, cold and disapproving, and my intestines turned heavy and knotted inside my belly.

At fifteen, your body grew woman-sized. You showed me the new bras your mother bought you, scooping them out from your drawer and holding them against your newly plump chest. Your hips, no longer narrow and bony, pushed against the seams of our school skirt so that girls stared as you walked down the hallways, their eyes hungry with jealousy. You were one of them, although you did not yet know it. Each morning, you snuck your mother's beige lipstick onto your lips, and smiled at your reflection in the mirror. You were a dot-to-dot puzzle, finally connected.

Unlike you I remained myself, a boy-child scrambling spider-like after my brother's friends, enviously watching them hoist their tall, gangly limbs onto the roof of our school. Our friendship became a covert affair. You pushed me to the edge of yourself and I waited patiently with all of you held in my inadequate, lonely hands. The sleek, well-proportioned girls with creaseless skirts and pencil thin ankles who invited you to sit with them at lunch peered disdainfully at the flecks of dirt caught in the ridge of my collarbone, my straggly, knotted hair, the sweat leaking from my forehead and onto the freckled bridge of my nose.

"Do you have to wear that?" you asked me one morning. We were sitting on the brick fence in my front yard. I looked down at my clothes—a chocolate-stained T-shirt and frayed, blue trousers that used to be my brother's—and shrugged.

"I don't know why you just don't dress like a normal girl," you said. "It's hard enough for us as it is, with our weird names and stinky lunches. Why would you want to make things harder for yourself?"

Because these are the only clothes that make me feel like I belong inside my own body, I didn't say. Because when I wear my school dress, I feel like a monster lurching between classrooms, I don't say. Because I want to peel off this road, crash through backyards and run and run until I reach the riverbank where we can play mermaids and pirates and pretend this will be our life forever and ever and I can't do that in a stupid dumb skirt, I don't say.

At school, with your friends that were not mine, you changed your name so that the syntax arranged effortlessly on their pink, perfect tongues. The syllables spilled out swollen and wrong and I trembled with the knowledge that you had wrenched yourself out of your own body.

But sometimes, in the middle of night, you would rap your bony fingers against my window, soft and featherlike, but I always, always heard. These were the nights when your father came home with a decade of toil roiled unsatisfied in his gut, choking on feelings that didn't fit down his greasy, dust-filled throat. My bed creaked as you eased your body next to mine and slid your arms around my middle, your heartbeat thumbing the space between my shoulder blades. And when I whispered I loved you, I swear, I swear, you said it back.

The first time you kissed me, we were lying, arms and legs splayed out on a sunbaked basketball court, pretending the rough surface warming our bodies was a beach we had never visited. Your new school friends never came here, but your eyes flitted about frantically every few minutes nonetheless. I swallowed the bile, thick and heavy and shameful, down my throat. We nudged our sneakers loose, lifted our spindly legs above our torsos and flung the shoes over our heads, listened to them thump dully on the distant grass, like tiny heartbeats. You asked if I thought we would be friends forever. I didn't answer, just turned to gaze at your velvety eyebrows, your narrow nose shifting with breath, the patch of freckles like flecks of paint dusting your cheeks. I didn't answer because I didn't think I needed to. Of course we would. You were inside me then, second breath. You leant towards me, and I cupped your face with hands that were no longer inadequate, no longer lonely. Your lips brushed mine and I gave myself to you, opened myself up, a word awaiting definition.

You were sixteen when you got your first boyfriend. You met him at church. He was an altar boy, and you were responsible for carrying the big wooden cross down the aisle at the start of mass. He was two years older than you and worked part time cutting timber in the greasy hardware store two doors down from our school. On Monday and Wednesday, he caught the bus into the city to study law at university. His father was the local doctor, a tall, silver-haired man who sat straight-backed in the third row of the church wearing a smooth grey suit and shiny black loafers. All pepper and salt of the earth.

After the service, your altar-boy boyfriend Peter asked if you wanted to sneak into the priest's room with him. You sat side by side on the frigid, wooden floorboards, passing the box of communion wafers back and forth and taking hesitant sips from the bottles of red wine stashed in cardboard boxes beneath the priest's desk. Late morning light turned your skin green and blue as it streamed through the stained glass window. When he kissed you, sliding his man-sized hands under your best pink dress, you called it the perfect moment even though that very morning you had pushed me up against your bedroom door and ran your tongue, wild and feverish, along the side of my neck.

Your parents earned a new church seat, next to Peter's parents. Your father caught the train to the closest department store and spent his entire weekly salary on the cheapest suit he could find. It was dark blue and too big for him. He kept tripping over the cuffs of his pants and had to use a paperclip to roll up his sleeves. He couldn't afford dress shoes, so he wore his torn Dunlop's, the only black shoes he owned. The sole had half fallen off the crumbled bottom of his right shoe and it slapped noisily on the polished wooden floor as he shuffled, head bowed, to his seat.

Every day after school, you met Peter at the hardware store. I came with you at first, breathing in the sick smell of wet paint and wiping my clammy palms on my itchy school skirt as you wrapped your pale, mosquito-bite-free arms around Peter's torso. When you folded your plump, perfect lips over his, I bit down on my tongue so hard the skin cleaved open, and blood pooled against my gums. I didn't come with you again.

The weight of getting older stoops my shoulders, hunching them against my hard-backed office chair in the city. Hot air pours through open windows and settles still and heavy above my neck. My scarred feet squirm desperately inside narrow ballet flats, aching for those sun-stained streets of our childhood. The clatter of a hundred typewriters is a butcher's knife slicing clean through my skull. I hate my job. I long for the crackle of dry dirt beneath my blistered toes.

On weekends, I catch the train forty minutes to the place we grew up. I sit straight backed on my parents' moth-eaten sofa and absorb my mother's stony-eyed disappointment. I am edging towards 33 and I am not married. I have no children. I earn practically no money. I am everything an immigrant doesn't want in their child: I do not, cannot, will not, fit in.

My mother asks about you only to emphasise all the ways she wishes you were her child instead of me. You live ten kilometres from me, which is to say we inhabit entirely different worlds. You serve camembert and olives to tall, eloquent lawyers and their shrill, Sunday-roast-cooking wives every Friday night. Your house has two-storeys with an oakwood front door and perfectly trimmed hedges. You married Peter, of course. You invited me to your wedding, but I didn't, couldn't, wouldn't attend.

I wonder if you ever think about the time I waited for an hour outside your bedroom window, rocking back and forth on the balls of my feet. We were supposed to go down to the basketball court—the place where you kissed me the first time—and eat the packet of sour straps I'd stolen from the lolly shop. Eventually, the screen door screeched open, and your father stepped out onto the front porch.

"She's at Pete's'" he said proudly. Pete. Hate, new and feral and burning, burrowed into my heart and refused to let up. The thought of you decades on still pokes at the wound, festering and gangrenous.

I see your father sometimes when I visit home. He is hunch-backed now, his hair needle thin and cloud-white. When I pass him (me, on the way to the shops to pick up milk for my parents; him, making his afternoon trek to church), he bobs his head in acknowledgement. His English has improved a lot, my mother tells me.

"He spends a lot of time with the grandkids," she explains. Before I return to the city, I trudge down to the creek, barefooted so that my long-ago torn heels collect all the pebbles and prickles scattered across the yellow grass. I pick up the cans, gum wrappers and damp socks scattered across the bank and cram them all into a plastic shopping bag. In cleaning the creek, I preserve it, which is to say, I preserve our child-selves and the games we played here. I run a finger along my striated palms and whisper your name—the name you no longer use—to the dry leaves rustling in the hot afternoon wind.

Lara is a third year Arts/Law student undertaking an extended major in English Literature. Lara enjoys buying more books than she has time to read and drinking far too much coffee.

$288m^2$, 3br / 18 Sommar Road

ELISE HO

This stately flaxen house offers unparalleled suburban experience on Sommar Road! With a location priding a whopping 16th on Safest Suburbs back in 2013, this ample 288m2 single-storey plot with 3 bedrooms and 1 bathroom is your paradisal starter home if you started with nothing! Arrive at the entrance for an early-access viewing of the property's temporary resident and her oily squid-ink hair. You can see her now, storming out for her big grandma being carried down the driveway, but can't hold herself farther than the house. You watch the Granddaughter chanting with the cheer of a Korean-idol fan, —BRING HER BACK BRING HER BACK—

In the stretcher Grandma reclines, two paramedics raising and clicking the bars either side.

—BRING BÀ NGOẠI BACK!—

Encounter the property, passing the off-white steel fence... stray white pebbles from the metre-long strip of garden bed. Your ankles appraise the driveway and wobble when stepping on it. The concrete sports some zigzag, corroded wear...

—BEGGING YOU JUST BRINGHERBACK PLEASE BRINGHERBACKSHE NEEDSTO EAT DINNER ATSIX!—

—But you'll re-lay the cement over the driveway, yeah?— Your husband asks, the two of you having balanced your way across the driveway and up to the front door.

Granddaughter at the front door stops with a twisting cut through her lungs.

You and your husband have trekked through the property's plant chaos in plastic pots, mounted the doorsteps. The front door is paired with a medium Mary statue on the pedestal.

Granddaughter buckles, her elbow rolling off the doorknob as she heaves with contorted lungs till sooner there's no more screeching rasps. She stills her stance, raising her gaze at your husband, —What?—

—*We've got our first little rascal along the way, you see*— He pats your belly. —*Don't want our baby getting bumps from anything poking out or uneven...*—

At the front steps, your husband nudges away the heavy arm of a potted jade plant. It bounces back at him. He hastily asks the girl again. —*You plan on fixing before selling*?—

Observe Granddaughter's eye pupils from her puffy eyelids, flitting back and forth, right to left. Granddaughter's searching for dizzy ambulance sirens, the current screaming situation suddenly slipping out her mind, but the only thing she seems to notice shining is a liquidy warm glaze which has descended, confusing her sight.

—*BÀ...*— She jerks. She stops. —*I*— She hushes herself, —*I can't fix...*—Then Granddaughter straightens her spine, regarding her visitors at the front step. —*I can't fix the driveway, but if you kill the weeds in the cracks... that'll make it look good... I think*—

—*Let's inspect inside the property, shall we*?— Your husband prompts, his creased forehead resting heavy on his brow. Your husband works in building management and likes chairing meetings. —*Today's open house. We'll start with the front*—

Kindly disregard any previous outburst from the teenage seller. Enter through the front door and be stunned immediately by the train-compartment confinement of the one-wall-kitchen-combined dining—its bonus function, an insulin clinic where this morning Granddaughter would've prick [sic.] Grandma's finger in the next hour. Yellow splashbacks and language barrier have been recently refreshed with tunes of the Aussie alphabet theme. Spectate the TV stuck on Kids' channel like the orange-juice cup rings sticky on the table vinyl.

Granddaughter comments here how she and Grandma sometimes laughed together watching Teddy on TV. Granddaughter doesn't tell you, though you learn from Blu Tack scars on the plastered walls, that other times they barely knew each other. With indulgent features including ten litres of fermented garlic in honey and tiger-balm-induced migraines clawing the freckled ceiling, this entrance will enthuse your visitors into pinching their nostrils as younger Granddaughter once did when Dad enforced biannual visits.

—Our understanding was that an adult... an elderly lady, apparently, was going to show us around— Your husband relays as he follows Granddaughter's squid-ink-spaghetti, loose hair sweeping her brownish arms, while you follow the back of his greying shaved head, the roll of his neck rubbing his polo collar. —You're not this property's owner— Your husband guesses of the girl. —Where's the usual guide?—

—She's... busy today...?— Granddaughter spots the insulin case flapped open beside breakfast. She scoots over, swipes it under the authentic redwood dining table and onto a chair—a flat cap hangs off the timber of the chair. *—Sorry—* she says. *—I'm just staying over. Please. Make yourselves... comfy—*

For a highlight in interior embellishments, Grandma's bodily accident that missed the toilet drags through the kitchen's travertine tiles in sepia, smearing strokes. You've been told by emergency services that Grandma on the driveway hasn't opened her eyes since Granddaughter found her spilling thirteen minutes before, like over-soaked mung beans.

At least the TV's still on. Teddy's tasting L for lamington!

Your husband cues, *—The next room, if you please?—*

Trace Grandma's naturally produced trail to the property's traditional-style and homespun laundry, some convenient three steps from the gas stove. The laundry has an indented washing machine strutting like a limbless robot, as well as a recycle bin brimming with spam letters obscenely mass printed.

—We predicted this, really— Your husband admits, pumping the diluted hand soap by the sink. He runs the tap. —Real estate always markets these places to look smarter th*an a doctor's smile. Can't know for sure until you've checked the place yourself—* He flaps his hands, flicks out the excess water which dampens the recycle bin, formerly a cardboard tray for bulk-purchased mangoes.

Granddaughter fishes out Grandma's past medical bills, slippery from the wet bin, mumbling to herself *—Why're they so hard to grip?... asshat—*

Your husband glances at the guide, —'*cuse me*?—

Witness Granddaughter pause, blink, say nothing to no one in particular, —Huh?— Seems she doesn't know what she just said.

Redirect your astonishment to the spectacular art curation in the laundry bin. One such showstopper is the paper sculpture inspired by the Dadaists—perhaps crafted and disposed of by Granddaughter herself. It's an envelope flap shredded to small bits vertically, reminiscent of kindergarten-constructed monster teeth! Its vivisected contents inspire equal intrigue—a birthday card from the government, their gift Granddaughter's right to vote. You don't know this girl giving you a house tour—can't decode more than what's commercially shown but the recycling bin's artwork knows. The toothed envelope in the bin knows that making decisions before Earth gets blown often makes Granddaughter binge *Easeyyfoodz* reels and her tears explode. Apart from the medical bills, Grandma's opened Centrelink notices abstractly frame the bin's edges, though you hear Granddaughter can't adequately translate the folded-A4 English for her (they call the phone service instead). Even if Granddaughter could, she would rather not be scalded by that bánh-xèo-maestro's *tongue* due to Granddaughter's chronically sloppy tongue or Granddaughter's slouched back... *straighten your back!*

The bundled laundry will also tell you how Dad dumped Granddaughter here, roaring that if she wasn't wiping her manicure nor planning to continue high school she could keenly turn into a tramp outside his investment. And the early weeks Granddaughter moved in here were welcomed *wholesomely* by Grandma and her *trời ơi, trời ơi...* under lukewarm light bulbs. Grandma hissed incessantly like the kumquat branch prodding the shutter above Granddaughter's pillow. Like the hissing hot shower on late arvos Granddaughter wailed and Grandma's hearing wasn't attuned enough to yank her out thrusting microwaved tea in her palms while wringing her hair through a towel.

But back to the open-house—your husband has left a property review!

—*The pressure's shockingly superb.*— Your husband rates, having teleported from the laundry to the nautical-palette bathroom, standing in the running shower. He's always sung like a fresh dreaming graduate in an old man's brass. —*Where'd she go?*— Under the black-crusted shower head, your husband's feeding his hair and polo shirt in dark, sopping weather. —*Where's our youthful estate guide? The girl?*—

You last saw Granddaughter knelt by the rhombus washing machine in the next room, the laundry. Door ajar, she's there still.

—Don't know,— she says now, the medical letters pouring from her hands. *—... don't know where I am.—*

The curled tongues of poured letters tell you that Grandma was bound by compulsory duty to a cracked bathroom mirror of a Granddaughter, while Granddaughter gorged on Grandma's accrued spoils, decades of sewing and doing labour work. One o'clock in bed, Granddaughter understood enough of Grandma's mutterings to know. She knew enough her own grandma didn't want her here.

But after a year's prolonged visit, TODAY in this exquisitely stenchy home, Granddaughter can't get enough of here! Some other fogged-up version of her can be heard still stuck at the front door, squalling at the paramedics as though there was no open house worth worrying over nor property worth displaying. Her testimony that this place is the place to be: —SHE NEEDSME DON'T TAKEHERAWAY FROM ME!—

Your husband ditches the shower stall, drips back into the laundry.

Granddaughter's cry for her favourite wrinkly queen would sure add heat to this laundry's humidity.

—Take us to the back— Your husband says. He shudders wetly. His Brogues bite the laminated flooring, masticate Granddaughter's scales that are the split letters flooding. *—Properties are like mullets... always trim in a selfie but you need to see the back. Show us the 'do at the back—*

Amuse yourself with the laundry's metal-mesh door too diagonal to fit in its frame, slants itself towards the backyard veggie patch, the back porch. Though from the soppy slap of paper, Granddaughter obstructs the door. *—No—*

—... You're blocking me?—

—No visitors past this point...—

—This is an open house. Sweet girl, you're joking. Don't you want to sell this building?—

—I DO—! I don't... I don...?—

—You said so yourself— And your husband hauls open the single-door and tall-standing cabinet, chucks out the downvoted brands of bleach and laundry powder, someone's crab pots. *—You're staying over. You're standing in for that Asian gran and this outdated house. You're only*

staying over— He seizes the fan straw broom leaning beside the disassembled toilet rails planning to be garden stakes while you stand away, your hand over your belly, and he re-sculpts the washing machine with battalion sweeps. *—This! Isn't your property—* And with friction of his collared neck, his roll of skin burns red. *—Tell me, IS THIS YOUR PROPERTY?—*

—I don't know, I don't kno...—

—Come on— Your husband kicks the back door, having shoved Granddaughter aside with the pressure required for hard-closing drawers. *—We're a good family. Doing a good thing inspecting this place as prospective renovators.—*

Skip through the kitchen-dining-diabetes-centre, past the old man cap to claw open the durian skin, savour the property's inner perfume, get deeper into the house. Sizzle after the perfect shower to slurp up the estate's scandals. Go deeper in the house.

—Come on!— Your husband mandates. His height takes up four-fifths of doorframes. *—Show us the back.—*

You bare the house open, open its memory, you rid the knots of laundry and you launch out through the bashed-metal door into someone's memory of bare feet landing onto the back porch.

The beige leather couch outdoor on the back porch enchants aliens and home pigeons for a mild snooze as the orange sun alights the horizon of eucalyptus, the ambient air spiced with grass ticks.

You know now this staple furniture is a fixture to the pumpkin-invaded backyard, its seat cushions ripped and ducted-taped thrice—a sunken, dust-ridden rift in time. Grandpa insisted he would order a custom replacement from the carpenter he knew thirty-something years ago, and Grandma trusted her husband would keep his word, forgot and waited some mornings for Grandpa to squeeze orange juice and croak his spiralling words.

Now neither of them will fix the seat cushion. No one tells you this. But six months after moving in, Granddaughter had curled on the couch, duct-tape folds pinching her black-soiled foot soles.

A second pair of foot soles, wearing thongs and crazed toenail paint, shuffled over the pigeon-crapped paving. Big Grandma sat, her bum weight converting the couch into a trampoline-seesaw.

As much as Grandma still climbed the roof to sort through the terracotta jigsaws, she wobbled with a mobility aid in the turbulence of her buffalo-son, his buffalo-daughter. Grandma swallowed ghosts, watching her children depart to different shores she could not follow, and even later once she landed on the same shore (sponsored to fly by plane), her one daughter and eight sons had elsewhere to go. Grandma let them, and she would do the same for Granddaughter—those sparkly manicures plucking Grandma's greys.

Grandma's sandpaper palm rubbed ripples over her granddaughter's back, her jade bangle knocking away the eighteen-year-old aches like a twig knocking across their steel, spear top fence. Whether Grandma inhaled Granddaughter deeply through her nose, watched her teeter over their driveway or accepted Granddaughter's bouquet of cut grass blades, she knew Granddaughter would fly from her as well. You don't know this. Granddaughter doesn't know either. It was like pouring water in cracked porcelain for Grandma to say she did not want Granddaughter here.

Must promise to herself. Granddaughter would settle. Granddaughter could sprout in another place better than here.

—But these memories will get wiped the moment this house is bought, right?— Your husband reminds in the open-house inspection. He wiggles his forehead crease at you, seeking confirmation which you give. *—It's not like we can keep the toenail clippings in this couch...or this couch, actually. I have some iconic furnishing ideas from the antique store we browsed.—*

But Granddaughter on the rotting wooden porch rattles her head. *—No...—* Granddaughter refuses. —We're still here. *Bà Ngoại and I liv...—*

Red-blue lights slice the backyard—

Through the tiny alley between brick and side fence, beelining from the house's front. Rays from the obnoxious ambulance crack the plaster across Granddaughter's eyes. And like TV cables unplugged from Granddaughter's throat, she grasps for breath. She chokes.

Excite your senses with apocalyptic wails of the siren. Peer back for the driveway and marvel at the stretcher being slid tastefully over the ramp, easily slotted inside the ambulance. Applaud Grandma's face as blue as the clear sky, her lips wrung out like fresh clothes in the hot breeze.

Granddaughter flies through the back, the meshed door detonating, stampedes from all the house's marketed compartments, chasing after the ambulance. Keep these soon-to-be heritage bricks manufactured by Blink & Co away from Granddaughter who wants to smash them with her fists but be also assured that no actual breakage will happen on this sturdy property, or *ever happen,* before selling! Feeling discomforted by all you've absorbed in this tour? Return all unwanted and foreign memories—guaranteed! You'll forget everything you've seen, will judge nothing more than what's before you of this building.

Today is the last day Grandma will see their brickhouse before it's sold. Something you won't know. Soon Granddaughter also, restored to slobbery screaming and scraping out dirt from jade plants as you follow her back to the front door, Granddaughter must also leave for someplace else. But for now...you jam with next-door neighbours playing radio's top hits. You nod at the council member taping the playground across the road after a kid with pliers snapped the swings.

The scaled Mary statue—Our Lady of La Vang tilts her round headdress over the permanent visitor, your young guide for this open-house viewing. Granddaughter can't follow her fleeing Grandma. Like an upside-down pilgrim down the house's stone steps, Granddaughter sinks.

—Gonna discuss this property with the unborn bubba— Your husband says, as you and him descend the house's steps. *—We'll let you know our decision next arvo... the ambo's making too much fuss. Your phone number, again?—*

He waits, saunters by the crumpled teenage girl soaked on the cement.

—Guess we can sort that out later.— Your husband stumbles over some scattered white pebbles then exits to conquer the next house inspection. Claim this plot for your lot and you'll be guaranteed the full amenity of a brisk ten-minute drive to Todder Public Hospital. Don't delay! Make this house your boat of family frenzy, the hope-sowed carriage over waves, your throbbing heart for home...

Elise Ho is a pre-service teacher who lives and plays on Wurundjeri Country (Melbourne). This is the second time she has written for Jacaranda Journal. She likes petting her bird and staring at her sucking catfish instead of working.

Interwoven

OLA KWINTOWSKI

The Tree

An ancient forest stands today as it did many centuries ago, filled with secrets and mysteries. The conversations within are carried through silences, by scent or pulsating signals. But sometimes the trees speak through the crackling of their roots. Should you be fortunate to pass through the forest at this time, you may be among the few who have heard trees truly speak. You may have stumbled upon their scheme to turn leaves toxic or make their bark taste bitter to ward off pesky insects. Perhaps they were conferring on whether to hold off seed production to starve ravenous boars obliterating their fruit in the spring, instead opting to flower the following year, to better their chances of replanting after predator numbers had lessened. Trees nourish their young and care for their sick— this is the way of the ancient world.

The day of the storm was just like any other. Animals foraged among the forest floor, ants crawled along the bark, birds hid in the canopy and vines stretched between neighbouring trees holding them tight. A sprig, bearing woody seed pods from a scribbly gum, was swept up by the wind. It shimmied into the sky, it whizzed above the trees, it danced along the wind's currents before landing atop the hill which overlooked the forest.

Rains came and went. The seed sprouted into a seedling, then a sapling and eventually a tree. The sun and moon took turns dipping and rising, seasons transitioned between themselves and eventually the tree grew tall.

Despite the tree being away from its family, they connected through their root system. They whispered during storms for it to bend and flow into the chaos rather than stand rigid and snap. When the tree was thrashed by winds, they sent it nutrients to mend. When the tree was scorched by the sun, they sent water for replenishment. Protected by its ancient family, the tree grew and thrived. However, on clear nights when frost clung to its smooth body and moonlight dressed it in a glimmering gown of silver, when the other trees cradled together, it stood alone and reached towards the stars. No matter how far it stretched, it never seemed to be able to touch them. It would be many years that it stood in solitude, till the girl arrived.

The Girl

She ran her hand along the warm, grey, smooth bark. Her school bag slumped by her feet as she turned her back to lean against the tree's body. She breathed in the aromatic eucalyptus and let the heat of the afternoon sun rest on her face. The warmth spilled over her and trickled into her soul. She loved being here. She'd always imagined this tree as the queen, overlooking her kingdom below, keeping a safe eye over her mob. She looked up and reached towards one of the lower branches and picked off one of the gum flowers. She placed it behind her ear. The flowers looked like exploding stars against the black canvas of her hair that cascaded down her shoulders. She closed her eyes and breathed in the silence.

In her left hand she held onto a crumpled note. There were only a few words scribbled in messy writing. But it felt as special as the secrets held by the universe.

The sound of a bicycle manoeuvring through gravel and grass broke the silence. A small smile crept onto her face. A beat passed; the bicycle dropped onto the grass. Slow steps approached the tree. Someone grasped her right hand, which hung by her side. Her smile widened.

She didn't want to open her eyes, afraid that her excitement would burst out and make the world explode. She bit her bottom lip. A magpie warbled above, making a fuss. Blinking her eyes open, ever so slowly, she saw his goofy smile before her—it put her at ease. He lifted his eyebrows twice as a hello. It made her laugh. Her heart beat wildly.

Hush, she whispered to it.

A gust of wind shooed the bird away and brought a gentle drizzle of the summer rain. They kissed for the first time. Neither of them knew it was raining, nor did they feel the cloud of moths that had been stirred and now swarmed around them.

She could smell the sweat on his skin, the woodiness of the tree, the sweetness of moisture in the air. Her head swirled and filled with stars making her feel weightless. The sugariness of the strawberry fizzer and cool mints exchanged between them lingered on her lips. Her chin was wet. It was gross. It was beautiful. She hoped the moment would last a lifetime.

They stood there a while. Their hands interlaced. Under their tree that reached for the stars.

The Stars

The Seven Sisters took council that night.

"Did you see the girl?" The first Sister asked.

"I saw the twinkle in her eyes," the second Sister smirked.

"Ooh, she got it bad," the third Sister chuckled.

"It's good to see the tree happy," the fourth Sister noted. "I've been watching that tree for at least a century now. Never seen it blossom so sweetly. I hope the girl stays a while."

"It's not the girl that's the matter," the fifth Sister chimed in. "It's 'em town folk. They been clearin' trees like they don't depend on 'em.'"

"Don't gettcha selves all attached. You'll blink and them humans will clear 'emselves before Sol is done watching over 'em," said the sixth Sister.

The seventh Sister was quiet. She liked listening to the others. Sometimes they would get so heated up a blue haze of energy would wrap around them. Surges of fire would splatter in all directions.

The seventh Sister enjoyed observing Earth from her vantage point and noting the everchanging landscapes— the rolling deserts, creeping coastlines, meandering rivers and islands that drifted along the oceans. She loved the interconnectivity between the landscape and its creatures, all made of stardust. But her favourite space was the one in-between—the space where stories unfolded, souls floated, and dreams wandered.

On a clear summer night, the Sisters had a brilliant view of the land. Earth's moon reflected Sol's ambience. The tree, on top of the hill, continued to stretch its arms skywards. On one of the top leaves, water pooled and reflected the night sky. The Sisters leant in and peered over for a closer look; the leaf caught their reflections. For a moment, they had all found their way to each other.

The Old Woman

She ran her fingers along the dark squiggly lines that adorned the tree's trunk. They looked like intricate tattoos. Tiny stories scribbled onto its body. She used to know how they were created. Something to do with moths. That memory was gone. Along with so many others. They sat behind fogged glass doors in the long corridor of her mind. She watched the fingers that stroked the tree. *Are those mine? So weathered and wrinkled?* Time had whipped past as fast as a tropical storm. It spared no one.

The tree was her pillar. They had both saved each other on countless occasions. She could no longer reach the lower branches as she used to when she was a young girl. A memory was making its way through to her of white flowers against black hair. A lifetime ago. A love ago. A heart break ago. Three words scribbled on a piece of paper. Three words that made her feel alive, invincible, happy. Then later, the same three words that fell short, were misconstrued and deluded. Her memories spiralled back into the fog.

She found comfort in the tree. No matter how lost she felt, she was always home with it. It was her heart on the outside.

The sun set as the chill crept in. She looked out into the crisp night. In the distance, she could see the Seven Sisters, low on the horizon. The fog in her mind began to clear. She had always felt the Sisters had looked out for her. She leant her back on the tree and watched as the dark of night enveloped the forest below. It occurred to her then, that the tree, like her, was the lost daughter of the forest being watched over by her family.

The old woman's hair glimmered under the moon, vibrant white against the velvet liquid of the night.

The fog rose once more.

Why is it so cold? She slid down against the trunk into a heap of leaves. They rustled and settled around her. She held one, dry and crumpled, in her hand.

The wind picked up. She breathed out a long closing white breath. It was visible in the night. It twirled around in the wind, it shimmied into the sky, whizzed above the tree and danced its way back to the stars.

Ola's writing is inspired by her love of art, literature, and the outdoors. She explores humans' entanglement and interconnectivity with nature to create ecocentric narratives that promote empathy and engagement with the environment. Her works have been published in TEXT, SWAMP, Social Alternatives, Verge, and reviews for Sisters in Crime.

7 Mandy Street

AMELIA ROGERS

When will you return? It questioned. Never? Never...

11:00 am

The little blue House, with its little blue door and its little blue roof, glared through the rear glass window.

Riley, with one hand on the steering wheel and one eye on the reflection, drove further away from the little House. The view of it becoming obscured as he rounded the corner. The boxes rattled as he took the turn. A whole life in boxes, a whole life in a boot and moving truck.

Riley began flicking through the radio. Pop song, host talking about something vulgar and inane, rock song, pop song, and that's enough. He flicked it back off.

By the time he arrived at his destination, the House would be sold, gone. The deal finalised and *7 Mandy Street* would be out of his hands. Never able to return.

He would never look out onto the rolling hills. He would never drink coffee on the veranda. He would never have Christmas in that House. They would never be together in that House again.

Never. Never. Never.

The words blared through the *empty* speakers; they bounced in time with the boxes in his boot as he drove over potholes. They jumped up and down inside his brain. He wouldn't swim in the creek, run through the macadamia trees, or eat at the local cafes.

His chest rose, up, up, up, or was that the car?

Although, he hadn't actually done that for years.

When he was a child, he would climb up to the top of the tree and call out for his Mum. She would come and talk to him as he shakily made his way back down. Up the tree was always easy because you knew where you were going, down you have no sight.

It was easier to drop when you were coming down.

Passing through the neighbourhood, the little houses blurred into the wide expanse of farmland. The farmland would eventually grow into tall buildings that covered the sky in grey. Riley tried to ingrain every inch of the green stretch into his brain.

The window was cold against his skin as he leaned an arm upon it.

8:00 pm

The sky began to darken as Riley approached his destination. A hotel above a Pub.

The Pub was loud when he walked in, backpack slung over one shoulder. There was a buck's party cheering and chanting in the centre of the crowd. The smell of liquor and booze was so thick you could drink the air. There was a live band on the small stage, three men singing an upbeat tune. They were pretty good for a Pub concert in this wayward small town on the side of the highway. A large man with a guitar and a singer with a long beard were belting into the microphone as the crowd at high tables cheered on.

Approaching the bar, Riley asked, "Can I check in here?"

"What?" answered the bartender, her voice husky as she leaned forward, a towel in hand wiping the inside of a glass. The bushy brown-haired lady was a larger woman, mid to late forties.

"I need to check in."

"Around the side," she pointed to the barrier breaking up the large Pub. Everyone in the small town must've been in this Pub. Riley shuffled past the bar stools and tables, elbowing his way through the crowds.

"Name?"

"Riley."

She took a large stamp and pressed it into the paper, *hmm old school.* "Here's your key," she dropped a real key with a keychain into Riley's hand before turning back to the awaiting customers. Riley headed up the stairs to his left, the noise of the Pub barely subsiding.

Room 19 stood in front of him; there was a swirl in his chest as he turned the key. Locking the door behind him, he took in the small room: a window that didn't open or close properly, mirror that looked suspiciously thick, fridge blocking the adjoining room, grey sheet covers. A bathroom with a green curtain, a yellow light, a cracked shower tile, and a towel rack falling off its hinges.

Sitting on the bed he took off his boots. The music from the Pub rang loudly through the wooden floorboards, the cold wind wafting through the gap in the window that lay permanently ajar.

Riley stared outside. The little town was positioned on the top of a hill and the Pub was located next to a bakery with big windows. In the morning, he could probably look out at the baker. *7 Mandy Street* had no fresh bread unless you wanted to drive for half an hour. The little House was in the middle of nowhere even more so than this. The chill in the room picked up. *7 Mandy Street* had a fireplace that warmed the wall behind it. Riley paced around the room. *7 Mandy Street* was cold, in the morning you'd have to wrap yourself in a doona to eat breakfast.

Riley turned the taps on in the shower, he couldn't seem to get it to stay warm; it was either icy cold or scalding hot.

11:30 pm

The bed was cold, the bed was crisp, the bed felt as if it was the coldest place in the world. Downstairs the music was loud, and the drunken buck's party mayhem raged on, but the band had finished up and cleared out.

The ceiling above Riley was white, bland. He lay staring.

12:00 am

The music had quieted, but the sound of people carried on. Riley put on his clothes, pulled on his boots and headed for the bar.

The room had mostly cleared out when he got to the bottom of the stairs.

"Last drinks," called the brown-haired lady that had checked him in. Riley took a seat at the bar.

"Lager," he nodded to the taps and crossed his arms against the bench.

She filled a glass to the brim and put it on the counter.

"What brings you here?" She asked, leaning on the counter. A group of people filtered out the front door laughing as they shrugged on their jackets.

"Room's too cold." Riley swigged his beer, the froth fast to evaporate.

"Huh, can't sleep?" Around the Pub was a small amount of people, an elderly man that had drunk too much and was struggling to keep his eyes open, and the buck's party. They were all slung solemnly on each other. Their faces earnest, their bodies drooping, one might misconstrue their mellow for a soft sadness.

"Mr Pitt! Mr Pitt! Oooh!" Shouted one of them, breaking the serenity as he stood and shook the guy's shoulders in a sudden burst of energy.

The sleepy elderly man's head shifted towards the table, but before it hit the bench, his hands slammed down, and he caught himself. He made a grumble against the bar and side eyed the group.

"Buck's party." The brown-haired bartender rolled her eyes as she polished a glass and set it on the shelf before picking up another one. "Marriage," she shook her head. "You got anyone back home?" *Someone back home?* The little blue House had seen it all. From his first kiss to his latest meltdown, it had seen everything.

"If you ask me, it's a waste of time," she said.

"Here," interrupted the old man, dropping a note on the table and stumbling for the door.

Riley took a swig, the condensation started to chill his palm.

The one getting married had rosy cheeks and glassy eyes. He didn't try to hide the grin smearing his face. He wore his "I'm Engaged" pin proudly. His life was about to change forever. The room felt colder than it had when he first came down the stairs.

"Thanks," Riley called to the bartender who was clearing the old man's glasses.

1:00 am

Back in his bed, the sheets were still cold, and *7 Mandy Street* was feeling further and further away. Riley closed his eyes; he was eight again, stuck in the tall avocado tree at the top of a perch trying to get down, except no one was there to tell him where to put his feet.

Amelia completed her Bachelor of Arts with a major in creative writing and literature in 2023 at Swinburne University of Technology. She is a writer with a penchant for enhancing the arbitrary and has been published in Other Terrain Journal and P.O.V collaborations.

Echoes

MATT MOORE

My arms rested softly on the smooth wood of the table; eyes focused on a half-empty glass. Condensation dripped down its sides, pooling atop the ceramic Rudolph coaster underneath. A fan blew lazily above the table, and green-trimmed napkins were buffeted by the air before floating back to the surface. In the kitchen, I could hear the chattering bustle of plates being taken from their drawers, and the clink of cutlery as it was piled into a container. In the lounge room to my right, the children sat on a pile of wrapping paper and boxes, a kingdom of their own making. New toys were strewn across the carpeted floor and leather couches, while grandparents watched on with quiet mirth.

I picked absently at my plate, taking the crumbs of pre-lunch finger food between my forefinger and thumb, and scattering them like seeds upon a bone-white field. A hand gently touched my shoulder and I looked up with a smile, leaning back against Adam, my head on his ribs. He wore a breezy button-up, his brown hair tousled and messy. Adam ran a hand through my curls, his fingers drifting over my neck as he leaned down to plant a soft kiss. I could feel his smile widening as our lips met, before the kiss ended and he stepped back.

"You okay?"

"I'm good. Did they need help in the kitchen?"

"They're almost done. I'm going to set up the music, okay?"

I nodded and took a sip of my drink, the melted ice having turned the scotch and soda mostly to water. Adam returned to the kitchen, and I leaned back in my seat. The noise in the other two areas seemed to deepen the void of the dining room, as though it were a liminal space, existing only between real worlds. The slip between two couch cushions. The minute space between clasped hands, or the pocket of air captured in a kiss.

This is where I existed for the moment.

I turned to the kids playing with their new toys and wrapping paper, and for a moment they appeared differently; now they were a young boy and girl, wearing Buzz Lightyear pyjamas and a turquoise nightie. They unwrapped their gifts quietly, and now I could see their parents watching on in mirrored silence. Polite "thank yous" were shared as the boy revealed books from underneath shiny golden paper, while the girl took a Cabbage Patch doll from a box, unravelling a white bow and letting it slide to the floor. There was warmth there, but distance too. An unseen divide that deepened with each lull in conversation.

The parents exchanged gifts with one another quietly, the father seeming surprised he'd received one at all. As the children left the lounge room, I blinked and felt a tightness take hold of my chest, pulling me back to the present. Sitting amongst the boxes and wrapping paper, the grandparents now played with their grandchildren, laughing loudly as they were told which toys they could play with, and the backstory for each crinkled element of the paper playground.

Noise drew closer from the kitchen, and I looked up to find the larger group entering the dining room. Adam's parents led the pack, each holding a precariously balanced tray, their cheeks rosy with drink and cheer. A few aunts and uncles helped set the table, clattering cutlery down on wood, replacing the used plates with clean floral ones. I stood to help but was refused with waving hands and claps to the shoulder as a plate was put in front of me. Despite the table's size, it struggled to seat every member of the Miller family—there were nieces, nephews, cousins, siblings, parents, grandparents and even a second cousin or two. Adam returned shortly with a Bluetooth speaker and his phone, focused on providing a soundtrack for Christmas lunch. He settled on *Harvest Moon* by Neil Young and placed the speaker on a kitchen shelf, before finding his seat.

Food was spread across the table—a trifle with a bottom layer of sponge, an assortment of bright citrus fruits and a lathering of thick, golden custard. A plate of sausages was positioned next to a loaf of bread and another plate of lettuce, tomato, beetroot and cheese. Homemade desserts, barbecue staples and—in the centre of the table—a large, honeyed leg of ham with a knife stuck in its side.

I felt the pressure return to my chest, as though someone was pressing the heel of their palm into my sternum. An ache made its home in my shoulders, permeating through my left side as my stomach started doing turns. As laughter and noise filled the dining room, my train of thought screeched against its rails, threatening to veer off the tracks entirely. I found myself at the centre of attention when Adam's relatives turned my way.

"How did you meet Adam?"

"What do you do for work?"

"Where do you see yourself in five years?"

I tried to answer interestingly each time, but stumbled over my sentences, fumbling easy responses, and turning away awkwardly as the conversation withered and dried. Adam was seated someway down the table, deep in conversation with his aunt about a reality show they both watched religiously. Feeling a twinge in my chest, as though a nerve was being pinched and tugged, I stood abruptly and left, taking my glass with me to the kitchen. Placing it on the island in the centre of the room, I folded against the marble, my hands gripped the edge and my head lowered between my arms. My vision blurred slightly as my lungs fought to catch up with my brain, thoughts and memories careening dangerously, caught in a gust of wind and flung around my head.

Looking up, I noticed the table seemed different—it was smaller, quieter. The boy and girl from before were seated at the table, though they were older. The boy had longer hair, and the girl wore glasses now. Their parents were seated at the table, talking quietly to another couple—the mother's own parents. Music played softly, and as the conversation died all I could hear was the scraping of cutlery on plates. The ample food looked similar to the Millers' spread, far too much for the people present. There were no decorations, no tinsel hanging from the walls, and no Christmas cards decorating the windowsill as there had been years before.

The distance had deepened.

I inhaled and felt my surroundings come back to me. Emptying the remains of my first drink, I poured another and regained my composure. Returning to the dining room, I found my seat and offered a smile to those I was next to— Adam's mother, Kim, and one of his nieces, who looked about six. Kim turned to me and leaned closer.

"So, Mark, where are your folks this time of year?"

"Oh, they're around. They live in the city, so not too far."

"Will you and Adam be going around there too? We don't want to steal you for the whole holiday."

"I think I'll see my parents tomorrow, but I won't take Adam away. I'm sure he'd rather be here with all of you."

Kim examined me for a moment, before looking down the table to her son and then levelling her gaze back at me.

"What makes you think Adam wouldn't want to come?"

"Our Christmas isn't really..." I paused, searching for the right words. My eyes settled on the Millers, their effortless cheer and togetherness. "It's not like this. It's just my parents, grandparents and Kate. It's not as fun."

Kim looked at me, a gentleness in her expression "You know, Adam told me he likes your parents a lot—and your sister. I'm sure he'd love to go."

"Thanks, Kim. I'm glad he likes them."

"He said you have uncles and aunts as well. Are they not around here?"

I regarded Kim for a moment, remembering Adam told me she was a guidance counsellor at a high school. My eyes glanced towards Adam's niece, Lucy, who was too busy fighting her brother over bonbons to be listening. I took a sip of my drink.

"My uncles don't speak, actually. To each other, or to us anymore."

"Oh Mark, I'm sorry. I didn't know."

"You don't need to be sorry; it happened a long time ago. They had a fight and I guess...holidays don't feel so much like holidays anymore."

"How do you mean?"

"Well, they're not like this. There's so many of you, but it's easy. There's no tension or awkward silences. There's loud music and chairs crammed in so everyone can sit together. Sorry Kim, I'm rambling—"

"No, no you're not."

I felt Kim's hand on my back, and the taut sharpness flooded through my chest once again. Her eyes seemed to search my face for something and, keeping her hand on my back, she spoke again.

"Not everyone's family looks like this. We're very, *very* lucky to have so many of us and to love each other the way we do. Your family might not be like ours but I don't think that's a bad thing. It's just different."

"It's nice being around all of you. I was thinking about when I was a kid and those holidays when we all still saw each other. Those times feel like...echoes. Like they're further away every time I think about them. Harder to hold onto."

"When you've lost something, it can be hard to hold onto the good parts. Just remember, loss leaves a space for something new. And Mark?" Kim moved her hand to my shoulder and squeezed warmly. "We love having you here."

Kim leaned around my chair, tapping her granddaughter on the shoulder. "Lucy, will you show Mark the toys you got?"

Lucy looked up, her eyes wide with excitement, quickly letting go of the bon-bon and causing her brother to pull back hard and smack himself in the face.

"C'mon, Uncle Mark! I'll show you where I hid the good ones." Lucy slid off her chair and took my hand, leading me over to the crumpled wrapping paper.

We sat on the floor as she showed me all the hidden toys, concealed in tombs of torn-up cardboard and ripped red paper. Lucy leaned against my arm, holding a few dolls and directing scenes as I played along.

This time when I looked back to the table, I saw my parents and sister sitting there. They spoke quietly, shared jokes, food and drinks. Their loaded plates weighed down the reindeer-patterned paper tablecloth, and the scent of cinnamon candles wafted through the dining room. I saw myself, too, telling my grandparents about what I'd been up to on my holiday.

I thought about how close my family were, how close we used to be, and how great the distance felt in comparison. That distance was still there, but the absence left a space to be closed, like a book taken from the shelf, making room for another.

This new book wouldn't be the same—its pages weren't as crinkled, its cover bright and clean. But there was time for a new story to unfold. Because those pockets, those voids left by absence, were filled with more of us. We were shaped by those absences. We couldn't be who we were without them.

I nudged Lucy and laughed as she made a joke, before returning my attention to the now full table. I met Adam's gaze and smiled when he stood to join us. Taking a seat next to me and helping Lucy into his lap, we sat shoulder to shoulder. I put an arm around him and tilted my head into the crook of his neck. I felt the question escape my lips before I could stop it.

"Do you want to come to lunch tomorrow?"

Adam's warm smile told me all I needed to know.

Matt Moore is a Meanjin/Brisbane-based writer, currently studying a Bachelor of Social Work (Honours) at UQ. Matt is interested in literature that reflects upon and explores the deeply personal, relating individualism to shared histories and experiences. When he's not writing, reading, or studying, Matt can be found playing D&D.

Convent

LILLIAN O'NEILL

i.
footprints left in sand.
crabs race to their hiding place—
I might just join them.

ii.
pig face's flowers bloom,
wilting neath the summer's heat
lilac fades to beige.

iii.
sea foam bunches, brown
now from man-made mindlessness
it was clear before

Lillian O'Neill is a creative writer based out of Meanjin and is in her final year of a Bachelor of Arts. Lillian primarily works within the forms of poetry, literary fiction, and creative non-fiction and often explores themes of female experience. Lillian is currently writing her debut novel.

The Limit

ANDREW MILLAR

You and I push out past
celestial fields, on up to Jupiter
where we perch upon the rocky surface.
From up here the earth rolls 'round the sun
so quickly—in fast-forward we re-live
two and a half years, so long-lived down there
and yet how the days pour out from our hands
like water or sand or so much earth,
where you and I gifted each other our time in space.
So many words passed from lips,
slipping into that deferring chain, never signifying
the true measure of feeling, instead usurped
in warm nightblue kisses on eyelids,
the soft smells of summer fruit hair;
a cheek offered up by my sweet girl.
No words lived in this domain,
that endless space, those days without end
where you and I grew
like two branches from the same Wisteria.
But any space fills, shifts shape to accommodate—
roots tangle, grow outwards,
leaving new routes laid down in soil,
until one day our boughs wave across the meadow,
in different forests,

on different saplings,
limbs reaching up for the constellated heaventree
of a night sky spread out like glittering wet pavement.
And for all that time,
in all those places,
we have seen the beginning and
we have been to the limit and
we have seen the stars change their course.

Andrew Millar is an emerging writer based in Brisbane/Meanjin, studying literature and philosophy. He writes poetry, fiction, and non-fiction essays. Andrew's work can be found in Jacaranda Journal, Exordium, Blue Bottle Journal, and the forthcoming issue of Meanjin. His never-ending project is a quest for a poetics of embodiment that feels authentic to lived experience.

Homecoming

NELL MCDERMOTT

My— our—
father

was born in this country
but it is not his and it is not mine

and your breath was not for him to bury
as Nan well knew.

Christmas lunch is as good a time as any
for the banished to return

reaching out long-fingered from the buffet
tapping gently behind framed panes of glass

You know your dad was married once before?
No—

Silence.
Shame-faced martyrs

set down plastic forks.
You died soon after.

I never knew you.
All I have are whispers
half-told stories, refracted memories

the static features of a stranger
in the photos that I find.

I try to picture you in prison
a blank-faced hunching shape

were you haunted by your exile
as I am by mine?

I never knew you

but we are bound by blood
an arbitrary connection

an uncanny absence
an embittered resignation.

I inherit the violence
of the newly unburied.

I inhabit the echo
of your middle name in mine.

I never knew you

but

I grasp your dispossession close.
I let it swell in my gut.
I make it my own.

Nell McDermott (she/her) is a PhD student in Creative Writing at James Cook University researching the relationship between machine-generated text and narrative time. She is the co-editor of Sūdō *Journal, and lives and works on the unceded lands of the Bindal and Wulgurukaba people.*

One Poem Written in Panic

IVAN DE MONBRISON

circumvention by random youth
cutting off all senses of measure
then cancer gnawing you
you held on to this limping butt
still burning on your
sad dried lips
it was a while ago
your small studio always filled up
by a thick fog
made of black tobacco smoke
you each night
frantically spent
pasting onto its ceiling
this poisonous cloud
while outside
in pitch dark night
skyless roofs kept on drifting
like motionless sceneries to forgo.

Ivan de Monbrison, French poet and artist. Published books in French include Les Maldormants hybrid text, illustrated, 2014; Irradié poems, illustrated, 2020; La cicatrice nue poems, 2020. Published in English: The Other Self poems, 2023. Swollen Bodies poems: due for publication this year by The Back Room poetry press (UK).

Root Cause

LAUREN M HANCOCK

Exposed roots,
barren nerve ends shoot
seismic shift
ache and flip
stake 'tween shoulders etched
blades eat at hidden labyrinth;
an entity unto themselves.

Metamorphose me into courage
rock, Oak to paper,
scissors
a winning hand amid apparent inertia
—seizure.

Eerie entanglement of supple tubers
amid ancient ancestors persisting for years—
hundred and one; lifetimes; stun.

Peeking past cast iron trauma
tender, parallel,
feet without wander
and I, a once-broken doll
am becoming erect, strong, tall.

In mind's eye I plunder against sufferance
the ties that bind me
Dare I alienate others?
Sick*amore* * is unimportant...
Self-soothe with liquid ease.

—Fierce stature—
To myself, leavening stark recovery
moored in time, dredged in serenity

Roots;
I dig onward.

---

*wordplay on sycamore: Sick love.

Lauren M. Hancock, poet from Melbourne, holds a Master of Teaching and a Bachelor of Music Performance. Lauren has published 'I'm sorry, but I think I still love you...', 'Keepsakes of Hope and Despair', and 'Our Whimsical World'. Lauren has also been published in Spillwords and The Poetry Lighthouse.

Maggot Shrooms

PARIS ROSEMONT

After Sylvia Plath's 'Mushrooms'

Maggoty cells are
Multiplying like
Plath's voiceless mushrooms.

Silently within
This dark breeding ground,
Spreading from my sown

Womb once they have grown.
Insurmountable
After their quiet.

Incubation—meek
Yet fierce—deceptive.
So many of them!

So many of them!
One would not even
Be aware of these

Maggoty mushrooms,

Till they come spilling
Out of my gaping

Mouth to take over.
Telling my story.
Their foot's in the door.

Paris Rosemont is the author of poetry collection Banana Girl (WestWords, 2023), shortlisted for the Association for the Study of Australian Literature's 2024 Mary Gilmore Award for a first volume of poetry. Paris delights in bringing poetry to life through multi-disciplinary modes of expression, and may be found at www.parisrosemont.com.

Baba Said

ANGELA COSTI

A house with no window
is an eye with no lid
the world's dirt gets in

I don't trust a painting
nailed to the wall
—a corpse in a coffin

Drill holes in my box
my wrongs are smart
—they'll learn from the worms

Angela Costi is the author of five poetry collections, nine produced plays/performance texts, and co-author of community book, Relocated. She travelled to Japan as part of an international collaboration involving her poetic text A Nest of Cinnamon. She is known as Αγγελικη Κωστη among the Cypriot Greek diaspora, her heritage.

Home, Body

ELLA KRATZER

Inside, my room is lined with shag carpet
So thick and dense I can grip it like hair
Rip it up like grass
Sink into the plush like sugar on milk foam
And fill my wet mouth
Until my insides are all wool and dust mites.

Outside, an apple tree squirms
With so many Christmas beetles
I can pick them like chestnuts
Feel them dig between my fingers
Scuttle up my neck
Until I'm bristling with chitin and hooked legs.

The bathroom sink is full of hair
There are no sheets in the hallway closet
Only cedar wood blocks and small animals.
I don't sleep, but I try
Lying still like the flies
Lined up on the kitchen table.

Ella is a 5'7" Leo made of all the usual viscera—blood, bone, meat and microplastics—with nice teeth and a self-inflicted haircut. She is currently studying a Bachelor of Arts in writing and received the Kingshott Cassidy Poetry Award in 2023. She hopes to fall in love one day.

Black Turtle Neck

THIRANGIE JAYATILAKE

I wanted to buy a black turtle-neck sweater
I thought I wanted to fit in
look like I belong at all the professional and art events
I turn up to
But
I am from sunshine and islands
I am from colour

a white person went to India
discovered colour
and now sells it as premium

you are premium
but I am sore thumb and confusion

I didn't know how to contend with living on stolen land
I was confused and out of place
I asked myself what is it

then I realized

I walk on streets named after colonizers

but never the people of this land
trams run green and yellow
the buildings it passes through
are not Aboriginal
I wanted to ask
Where did their architecture go?
Where are their sculptures?
Where is their art in the city?
Why is it still hidden?

then I walked into a park
and I saw the trees
little yellow flowers peeking at me
at least for now
there it was
my missing link

Thirangie is a Sri Lankan writer and editor based in Naarm. She writes poetry, fiction and feature articles. Written in a narrative prose poetry style, her poetry addresses social politics, nostalgia, place and memory. She has been published in Airport Road, Farrago Magazine, Myraid Magazine, Postscript, Gazelle, and Xenozine.

Unanswered Beginnings

VANESSA LEE

eighteen-year-old boy on a boat;
knife in hand, stand by strand.
loose hair dancing against moonlight,
swallowed by the hungry seas.
the qing dynasty follows.

trail of blood and rust of the past
grandfather, did your world smell of iron,
of dust?
sea salt in your eyes, hands trembling—
you must have washed yourself
of an old cast.

sample the aftertaste of a new beginning,
the loneliness of malaya begs and groans.
shed your leathery skin, snarl your teeth,
and begin anew.

your children, my father,
tell tales of an older man amid the fields.
through smouldering heat, another smile
(some fractured memory of a light-speckled lake)
under an unkind sun with blistered feet.

i wonder who you were.

passed from sibling to sibling
are fading scents of adored dishes,
gasps of static from an old favourite radio.
mere echoes of a haunted hometown
where light speckles amid an endless sky—
yet the memory still drowns.

Vanessa is a final year medical student at the University of Queensland, who dabbles with poetry from time to time. When the world falls away at night, she puts pen to paper with a cup of tea and writes away. She has previously published work in Farrago and Myriad Magazines.

Margaret

BREE TURNER

Sunkissed ivory bejewelled blue what skips a
generation can be bought in a box mud-like
mix smelling of earth and fish
hair dyed henna red

Margaret keeps auburn locks
in a silver chest
remembering her granny
Rubenesque and brazen

Before her father died she
promised to visit his mother
lux, fides, familia—light, faith
and family

Childhood was Vegemite and sand
dances 'Auld Lang Syne' on the
wireless
soccer Saturdays church

on Sundays

Somehow she missed

something she had never known
home and heartsick she boarded
a ship

Three years passed

She may never have returned
had she not written

her mother

her people

regaled in her travel stories she realised
quickly how little

had changed

She married a widower and
gave birth to a son though she
had always wanted a daughter

When her first grandchild was born she
dressed her in tartan and sang 'My
Bonnie Lies Over the Ocean' promising
to take her when she was older

Now in her eighties
bound by arthritis and
high blood pressure her
confidence to travel has
waned

Margaret's granddaughter made a
promise too

Riding along the highland boundary

she doesn't know anyone by name
but their faces

The lilt of their voices the
callous of their hands the
nutty taste of their food
this she knows.

Bree Turner, Ph.D, (she/her) is a social researcher and writer originally from regional Australia, currently based in Paris. Her research and creative practice often explores gender, relationships, digital cultures, and performativity.

Separate Lives[1]

ALISON J BARTON

startled buds spring from charcoal-dark earth
like precious fruits berries nuts
pods full of gushing essence
flanked by curved grids in segments that calm eyes

the sun's jolting spires are contained in a capsule
scarred clean with shadowed stems
and ovaries that form a woman's strength and vigour
a goat skull framed by wormed branches

a mother is in this ripped place
in clay black and white striated like labour
like pushing pushing birthing neverending lifelines
the artist ordering what cannot be ordered—a life-giv-
ing body

with wounds like what is damaged in the hidden
undergrowth of ripe Australian bushland,
also massacred ground
the bones and scars we share

part of the earth, of us
where we've tried to stitch back together

to repair defilement
the art of loss and re-birth reverberating

a tree renews from gas-smoke remains
spits of ash flying across
texted tablets now antiquities for setting the story
cementing the tale

the silver of a blade ekes out strips of curtain
designed to shade the evidence
as though the innocent could be shielded
from the shadowed grit mosaic

broken remnants are cracked and cracked again
then repaired so the break splits light open
what would they say seeing us now
everyone wailing

---

[1] Some words or phrases in this poem are lifted from original artworks by Karen Ami.

Alison J Barton is a Wiradjuri poet writing in Naarm (Melbourne, Australia). Themes of race relations, Aboriginal-Australian history, colonisation, gender, and psychoanalytic theory are central to her poetry. Her work has been published in Australian and international poetry and literary journals and she can be found at alisonjbarton.com.

Dear World Creator

OLLIE LANAGAN

"Make me, make me belong," I dare—
Not in the way where I am changed;
Not in the way where you erase;
But in the way where the earth is morphed,

Shaped beneath your hands like the soft
Putty that it is. Creating
Space, forging without taking.
A place for both me and the norm.

You sat, once, with skin and guts
Adorning your hand, and made me—
Made us—unique, ethereal.
Holy bodies. Wholly human.

Do you know what it's like, down here?
Other bodies, other beauties,
Seek us—seek that we become them,
Or drown us, dream us disappeared.

They deem us unholy, twisted.
Tell them, tell them we are yours, too.

Convince them we are your children.
That we are both as old as time.

World surgeon, watchful warden—
Please, show us where to feel at home.
Then, if an abyss is the only place,
Placate them so they leave us alone.

Ollie is a proudly queer Brisbane/Meanjin-based writing student. They love to write about their life experiences and feelings as a trans, anxious, and depressed person. In his spare time he plays video games and showers his two black and white tuxedo cats with affection.

Forest as Mise En Abyme

BRIDGET WEBSTER

I don't have to
close my eyes to see it—
your funny little hat
weaving through the trees
green melts the clearing
the living breath
of a wooden flute

we walk a soft meridian
cataloguing carbon
measuring dead sticks
that sometimes turn out to be roots

the light changes
and the forest licks its lips
how different feels the weather
getting cold and wet together
we set down our instruments
lie on milk moss
it is silvery and you like it best

above us the clouds
are scudding clots of light

and grandmother myrtle
carves lacy glyphs
in the changing clay of the sky

we're getting closer
the sun notices
motes of rain
start moving upwards
in a patient scale

slowly, as if
from an undiscovered Ghibli
the milk surface ripples
our forms suspended at the centre
a mirror film unfolds
across the retina
of the world

below
moss surges
a forest in itself
springtails ceaselessly
shiver and fizz
and grandmother myrtle
shapes ancient cuneiforms
casting her nerves
through the networked earth

motes of rain
move downwards
the same way your eyes
keep sliding from mine

we gather up our instruments

only sometimes it turns out
with a funny little fumble
we're grasping at a root
not a piece of debris

the mirror flips
everything
is more alive than we imagine

motes of rain
stand improbably still
you're looking down at my lips
and I am licking them

Bridget Webster writes on unceded Wurundjeri Country across poetry, fiction, non-fiction and for stage and screen. Her short fiction has been shortlisted for the 2023 Neilma Sidney Short Story Prize, and her poetry published and awarded the 2022 Emerging Poet prize by Liquid Amber Press.

Lost Currents

IBTISAM SHAHBAZ

there are voices with inflections
that walk across the room like a familiar beat
sights, sounds, smell
so many moments i have swallowed
only to become that girl again
sitting on a couch, waiting for a friend

forever waiting
for a copper to conduct this electricity
to charge my confusion in a medium who understands
yet the same cables that connected me
i snapped with serrated steel scissors
no current flows through me now
misdirected channels buzz a lost rhythm
some voltages just ran too high
burnt the socket they called home

so life has become flat again
a bronze statue rusts to brass
and like Midas,
i walk through the world in woollen gloves

afraid of the ones I might rust

Ibtisam Shahbaz is an emerging writer in Naarm. Her work is influenced by her Australian, Pakistani, and Muslim heritage. She has worked with Red Room Poetry on their annual Poetry Month and Poem Forest projects. Her fiction has been published by outlets including Monash University Publishing and Hawkeye Publishing. She is currently the Poetry Editor at Be:longing Magazine. You can find more about her writing journey at

Exposed Roots: An Interview with Rae White

SAFFRON JONES

I had the privilege of being introduced to Rae White at the 2023 Brisbane Writers Festival through a mutual friend after I had commented that non-binary writers and readers need to stick together.

Our chat wasn't more than a few minutes, not even landing on a particular topic from what I can remember, but Rae very quickly became one of the most personable and down to Earth authors I had met the Festival. A quick signing of a post-it note and an agreement that yes, non-binary writers and readers should stick together, was all it took for me to read through their most recent poetry collection *Exactly As I Am*, published through UQP in 2022.

And it stuck with me. My favourites are dog-eared at the top for ease of access or dog-eared at the bottom to return to later after letting the words sit. When potential interviews were raised for this issue, I jumped at the chance to reach out to Rae and ask the questions to learn more about their work and experiences as a non-binary writer.

Exactly As I Am was shortlisted for the 2023 Prime Ministers Literary Awards and the Judith Wright Calanthe Award within the Queensland Literary Awards. Rae's debut publication, *Milk Teeth* (2017), won the 2017 Arts Queensland Thomas Shapcott Poetry Prize, was shortlisted for the 2019 Victorian Premier's Literary Awards and commended in the 2018 Anne Elder Award.

As well as a slew of additional accolades, Rae is a warm presence at local writing events such as Ruckus Slam, on top of their founding of Uplift—a poetry hub uplifting people through community events and opportunities—and #EnbyLife—a journal for non-binary and gender diverse creatives.

Hi Rae! You have actually submitted to Jacaranda previously, an intimate piece titled *Dive in* that evokes the soft quiet of a once busy street now on pause, all its inhabitants breathing together. What brought about this poem, and how did you come to find Jacaranda?

I love your summary of this poem! I found Jacaranda through previous editor-in-chief Olivia De Zilva who encouraged me to submit something. 'Dive in' was inspired by the flooding in Meanjin that happened in early 2022, when my apartment complex became like an island surrounded by water. Because of the lack of traffic on the main road, I was able to hear incredible things I normally wouldn't, like the sound of my neighbour's dog breathing outside my window.

***Hussshhh* is a direct look into the mindset non-binary people enter whenever they go into a gendered public bathroom—beginning with a pre-emptive shying away from potential attention and then trailing out with quiet anxieties and unseen whispers—was this piece written in a spur of the moment, or was it planned out?**

That's exactly it! No matter whichever binary bathroom I go into, I'm always preparing myself for something: looks, questions, glares; even if they never happen. This poem was based on a moment at a writer's festival where I was feeling strong and happy in my gender identity, appearing at the festival as a non-binary trans writer, and then I found out there were no gender-neutral bathrooms. It felt like a de-gendering, and then someone questioned my place in the bathroom, and I knew I had to write this poem.

How did you come to decide that this piece should be fourth in the collection? Is that just how the editing cookie crumbled or was it more strategically placed?

Oh that's an interesting question! In *Exactly As I Am* I kind of bunched poems together in sections, dependent on the title/vibe/theme. The book is a journey through trans discrimination ('Exclude'); survival and resilience ('Exist'); defiance and resistance ('Exclaim'); taking up space and taking a breath ('Exhale'); and trans joy and love ('Exalt'). I wanted Hussshhh to be somewhere in the 'Exclude' section and I put it closer to the front because it was engaging and punchy, and also because I thought it might be a good entry point if people knew the poem already (it was awarded Highest Queensland Entry in the 2019 XYZ Prize for Innovation in Spoken Word).

to voyage with loved ones who transition is an ode to the quiet moments held between breaths and in the palms of those who are treasured enough to witness the exposed roots of a loved one's transition. Are you able to speak a little on those exposed roots and the communal support they might bring?

I loved writing this poem so much. So many of my beautiful loved ones are fellow trans people, and it's been a privilege to watch them grow and flourish. There's so much bad press around people transitioning—as if someone in your life coming 'out of the closet' and telling you a vulnerable thing about themselves is somehow a disaster, a punishment, a weakness. But I think it's the exact opposite! Someone you love in your life (a friend, a lover, a partner, a family member) telling you they're trans is the most beautiful gift, and a journey that I'm so proud to take with someone.

I have been lucky enough to unearth a copy of the fanzine you penned—No Horizons: A Dystopian 'Animal Crossing' Poetry Zine—of which tongue-in-cheek poems about the beloved video game are a must. However, smack in the centre of the zine is a genuine reflection on assigned genders at passport—the Animal Crossing equivalent of assigned genders at birth. Can you tell me more about the exploration non-binary identity through fan fiction, and the importance of zines in fostering community?

Oh I love Animal Crossing! I really enjoyed writing this zine because it allowed me to explore capitalism, colonialism and gender binaries in my fave video game. I have written a bunch more poems since then, so I'm thinking there's a Volume 2 of this zine in my future.

A lot of video games try to be flexible with gender but just end up reinforcing binaries—like in the case of the English language version Animal Crossing: New Horizons where at the start of the game you have to choose a 'style', which is either long or short hair. Your character can still wear whatever clothes they want, and they can change their hair throughout the game, yet still there's this underlying little niggling implication of "but what are you really?" I think that maps to societal expectations of gender in Western society. No matter how non-binary I am or feel, someone will always want to know about assigned gender or genitals even though, at the end of the day, it's not relevant to how you treat someone, and it's also a completely made-up social construct.

Zines are fantastic! I love how zines have this low barrier to entry and there's no hoop-jumping like with more traditional publication pathways, so if you've got a cool idea or some poems you've penned you can pop them in a zine and print some off, and you're sorted! Anyone and everyone can make a zine and I think that really fosters beautiful communities full of self-expression and exploration.

Lived experience presents itself on our bodies—we carry things with us, showing it in how we move and interact with those around us. Do you think words might hold similar weight, becoming our inked-to-page bodies in a newly realised transition?

Oh what a cool concept! I do feel like there's a such a tactility to both printed poetry and the body, and I definitely try to play around with the form and structure of my poems to make shapes like bodies (e.g. 'two figures') and explore the space of the page. For me, at least at this stage in my life, I find that my words and books are sometimes adjacent to record keeping, to cataloguing my lived experiences and writing myself into our trans history. In that sense, I love the idea of my books being with other books on shelves, sharing bodily space in archives with other trans stories.

The subject matter of *Exactly As I Am* is very starkly and unflinchingly trans—in the past, have you had any difficulty with editor perception and reception of your work by the public?

Honestly, it's been pretty good! My agent Danielle Binks and my publisher UQP have always been hugely supportive. At readings or in public, there's sometimes misgendering or confusion about what non-binary is, but most people have been on board once they know

I'm trans. I've definitely received some hate mail, but I mostly get lovely messages from people who've really resonated with my work and that's an absolute joy. I'd be prepared to block hundreds of transphobes on social media for just one 'thank you' from a fellow trans person. It makes it all worth it.

What has been your experience with submitting trans works to cis editors?

I've mostly found the experience to be a supportive one, especially with my two poetry collections. In terms of one-off poems in journals and magazines etc., I usually submit my work in good faith, with the assumption that every editor is trans friendly and a lovely person. And they most often are! I'm sure some editor has rejected a poem of mine for their journal because they're a transphobe, but that's a them problem, and I wouldn't want to be published by them anyway!

Often, trans and non-binary writers find themselves pre-editing their works—sometimes before the words even hit the page—so that themes and nuances of identity can become more palatable to wider audiences, have you, or do you, experience something similar? If you do, how do you overcome it?

Ohhh that's an interesting question! I don't censor myself. I don't feel the need to answer to a particular audience or to a cis gaze, and I couldn't care less if someone doesn't find my work palatable. But that being said, I do try to write my work in an accessible, approachable way—so that even if a particular theme or something might be daunting or confronting, it's still written in a way that people can understand and vibe with. I think this is especially important now I've started writing manuscripts for younger audiences.

With publishing's increased focus on diversity and inclusion, do you feel there is greater and more permanent space for trans and gender diverse works in the Australian literary sphere?

I definitely think so! I think we're really making our mark, especially with recent trail blazing books like Nothing to Hide and Transgender Australia, and there are more and more gender diverse works being published every day. Nothing's perfect, especially when capitalism is involved, but I know so many passionate people who work at publishers who want to publish work by diverse voices. That makes such a huge difference. So, I remain hopeful that trans folks are carving out a permanent space within Australian publishing and I look forward to seeing what's published next!

In the past, and even currently, have you ever struggled with finding a place or publication for your works that deal with gender identity?

My agent and I have definitely had our fair share of rejections (there are unpublished YA and middle grade books sitting on my computer just waiting for their time) but I've found that rejections of any kind, for either manuscripts or single pieces of work, are most often about subjectivity of opinion, the work not meeting a journal's theme or vibe, or the fact there's heaps of work out there and not enough publishers or money etc. It can be about so many things, and in the majority of cases I choose to take rejections and editorial feedback in good faith. (I actually wrote a zine called Dealing with Rejection in the Arts!)

Through your experiences in traditional and non-traditional publishing, have you noticed any shifts in how trans works are received by the public?

I think I live in a little bubble a bit because poetry isn't that widely read, and I attend a very queer book group! But I do think that trans work is being published and read more. We've always been here throughout history, but we're definitely being 'seen' a lot more at the moment. And in reaction to this, vocal minorities, anti-trans legislators and general assholes love to pop up out of the woodwork to ruin the party through their book banning and bigotry. Sucks to be them. They don't get to read beautiful books about beautiful trans people, and they're all caught up in their hatred. Their shitty opinions ruin trans lives and I will never let them win. Maybe I'll feel differently once my kids picture book is published (All the Colours of the Rainbow is being released with Hachette in 2025!) because I am a bit cautious about the hate I'll receive. But honestly, I reckon if you're trans and something you write isn't received well by the public then they don't deserve you! And if you're trans and you're getting heaps of rejections, consider self-publishing or make a zine or similar. You got this and I believe in you!

You're very involved in the literary world and community, holding multiple professional positions and running Uplift, a hub for community activity, and founding #EnbyLife, a journal for non-binary and gender diverse creatives—do you have any advice on becoming involved in your local literary community?

I love community so much! I reckon the key is to attend events (in person or online) and chat with like-minded folks. It can feel daunting, but it definitely gets easier. And if you're finding there's not a community you vibe with, you can always start your own. (Which I acknowledge can also be hard for neurodiverse folks, disabled folks etc and I know I'm hugely privileged to be an extrovert brimming with executive function!)

Do you have any final, closing remarks on the strength of sensitivity that exposed roots hold?

Community is all about roots and resilience and growth, and so I want to encourage creatives to find their communities. If Uplift (upliftpoetry.com) or #EnbyLife Journal (enbylife.net) interest you, then check them out! At Uplift, I send out newsletters and post on socials with events and things people can get involved in, and we also have our own upcoming poetry events. And if you're looking for a particular type of event, group or poetry book or something, send me a message on Instagram or wherever. I love connecting people with communities and seeing folks thrive!

I would like to thank Rae White for their time, energy and words, both for this interview, throughout their published works and their founding of Uplift and #EnbyLife. I would also like to thank my fellow non-binary Jacaranda Journal editor Jack Antony (he/they) for contributing to this interview. There is a great and welcoming community of non-binary creatives in and around Meanjin, I am thankful that my own roots have found a place within.

Rae White is a non-binary transgender writer, educator and zine maker. They have published award-winning poetry collections Milk Teeth (2017) and Exactly As I Am (2022) through UQP, as well as founding #EnbyLife, a journal for non-binary and gender diverse creatives, and the community poetry initiative Uplift.

Saffron Jones is an emerging non-binary lesbian editor and writer based in Meanjin. When they're not procrastinating their studies, they're trying to not become a two-coffees-a-day person while hanging out with their three cats—Oreo, Breulei and Chunky Beef. Saff is passionate about supporting local writers and writing communities.

One in Eight

CHRISTINE BURROWS

My neighbour went down to the Reservoir early to toilet his Westie. Got back as I was heading down there to run my little black dog. Told me, "big crowd doing the breast cancer walk, hundreds of them, hot pink tutus, ribbons everywhere."

Sudden cold armpit sweat prickled like tiny knives and my heart throbbed like a kettle-drum as the scene unfurled in my head:

> families, workmates, Tittie Sistahs; lycra-jogging, strolling, striding, straggling; entangled dog leashes, oodles yapping at rescue hounds; big-eyed babies in slings and strollers; nuggety toddlers on push-handle trikes obstructing mobility scooters, with pink flags flapping; Breastie T-shirts and pink ribbon glyph-emblazoned merch uniting the disparate crowd buzzing with camaraderie, belief in making a difference, daring to hope for a cure.

See-sawing between Freeze and Flight, the fulcrum of Fight collapsed into a hellish imagining of the sensory overload of colour and things and faces and feet and noises and smells and feelings and breath, jagged breath and counting heart-beats (if I count slower will the tempo drop while simultaneous thoughts shunt together, perilous, in a cracked moment) losing, losing, losing the plot and my trauma so fresh and, radiation burns still painful. I would pollute the buoyant community spirit.

I would scry faces, look for signs:

Are you one of us, the survivors: the scarred, the scared, the sacred? Are you in treatment? What H ell has it taken you to? Do your legs burn, does your skin itch and weep? Have your radiation burns healed. Did your hair grow back curly? Are you in pain? Of course you're in pain. Can you eat? Can you sleep? Can you remember? Can you laugh before you cry again? Can you lift your head, your child, a bag of groceries, your lashless eyes to god or the mirror? Is anyone holding you? Did your mother wife sister daughter aunt granddaughter, grandmother friend colleague neighbour kind stranger - die? Vale. Oh! I am so sorry. Are you, ok? Are you a one in eight woman?

So I swivelled away from walking towards the Reserve, pulled at my dog to go in the opposite direction to the forest where there would be no-one and nothing but trees, scrappy ironbarks, stunted blue gums. Roots with tenuous purchase in the mullocked, pock-marked ground, run horizontally, lumpy and stringy, tracing fissures in rock and cracks in the earth. Nonplussed, the dog trotted alongside, jaunty as ever, tail waggling.

The next day we took the usual path to the Reserve, finding solace as always in the plethora of colourful eastern rosellas, assertive magpies and cheerful galahs just doing bird things in the trees, creek and scrubby ground. On the smooth walkway circling the Reservoir there were heavily pink-chalked messages in letters large enough it spans its width.

YOU'VE GOT THIS!
THINK PINK!
CANCER'S TOUGH BUT SO ARE YOU!

The kettle-drum thumped PA-DOM PA-DOM in my heart and my head. Seized by an urge to scream and never stop, I recoiled from the path as if from a monstrous snake poised to strike.

But I didn't scream, of course I didn't. No. I collected the shards that shock had scattered and stepped over the things that people say when compassion and fear tie tongues in knots   while cancer snaps at our heels like the dog of the Tarot's Fool. Maybe next Mother's Day we'll lap the Reservoir with the allied throng. Me and my dog, in pink tutus.

Christine resides on Dja Dja Wurrung Country in Victoria with a small black dog. She writes poetry and creative non-fiction, these two styles often blending as she explores themes of trauma, dislocation, and environmental justice. Her work has appeared in Cordite, Landfall, Westerly, Audacious and Australian Poetry.

Rose Garden

STEPH MAKER

I'm covered in scratches. Some are deep. They look a little frightening. Especially the cranky ones near my wrist. I know I shouldn't make light of it, but I can't help it. I come from a long line of people disposed to gallows humour—it's a deep-rooted survival mechanism. I often joke to my colleagues, telling them not to worry about me: "It's not self-harm, ha-ha, just risk-taking behaviour."

It's probably neither. That's certainly what the good people on Gardening Australia would argue. They assure viewers that pottering about outside is health-giving and relaxing. But that argument doesn't strike me as the full story. There are certain elements of gardening that deviate into monastic self-flagellation. Dare I mention hand weeding? And, indeed, after my last bout of pottering I *was* bleeding.

On the weekend, my partner and I tended to our roses.

My favourite rose is in a bad place. Maybe I am too.

It had done its best. It pushed out one flower. And it was brilliant: a deep violet, with an abundance of petals. It is my favourite. I am still learning about plants, but I know enough to decide that this rose would do better with more sun. Currently, it's shaded out by a weedy palm and a crumbling rock wall.

A quote comes to mind, that has become an inspo-meme: "When a flower doesn't bloom, you fix the environment in which it grows, not the flower." I can't help but groan. I roll my eyes at myself for letting such an asinine self-help axiom resonate with me. I am sceptical of most expressions that pop up on Pinterest boards as image macros with clear typography on landscape backdrops.

Still, I'm moved by the pinspiration. I waddle back inside. *Ugh, I guess I'll fix the stupid environment.* I kick off my thongs and pull on my gumboots. Despite my prickly mood, I fetch the good shovel and resolve to move the rose. *Look at me taking responsibility for my surroundings like a fully formed adult.*

Our home used to be—as I understand it—a bit of tourist trap. Whenever we meet our neighbours, they invariably say, "Oh, you're the ones that bought the Rose Cottage." They share lore and gossip about the property.

"It used to be a nursery!"

"It was on Better Homes and Gardens once!"

"Did you know the wife ran away with the gardener?"

"Would you believe that when the original Rose Cottage couple sold up, people snuck in and pinched all the good roses?"

It is delicious.

The property had changed hands a few times before we got to it. I feel a strange gratitude to the couple we bought the place from. They let it go. They had bigger problems to manage: a difficult teenage son and a failing relationship. They left cars, shipping containers, and caravans to rot on top of the grass; now, the lawns are dead. We fought with the valuer because he said the place was uninhabitable due to a half-finished space intended for a laundry. If the place were in top spec, we'd never have been able to afford it. We are lucky. Fortunate. Privileged.

We get to live here because it needs love.

After Dad died, Mum went on a memorial rose shopping spree. Without context, the volume of plants she bought would have appeared manic. She'd have left the nursery with a car boot-full. But family just kept dying: first my aunt, then my dad, and those of us who were still alive had to do something. She did the things you do after your sister-in-law and husband pass.

Of the living—post-funeral especially—we lean on Mum as the person with a bias towards action. She's easily the most competent and the least likely to be paralysed by pesky feelings. That, of course, is not to say she isn't feeling, mourning, grieving; but, in doing so, she's also able to pull her finger out, breathe, and move. She is a force.

She bought: one dad-rose for her to put in her garden. I think she has an aunt-rose too. Another dad-rose, and another aunt-rose, for Nan to plant in the churchyard. And one dad-rose for me. She purchased a rosebush for me to remember my aunt too. I can't remember whether she explicitly stated an intent or meaning for the one with the striated pink and yellow petals. And a bonus one...because...well...we're that nice young couple that bought the Rose Cottage. We are neither nice, nor particularly young. But, whatever.

Several forces have culminated, leading to my partner and me standing in the yard ready to plant a formal rose garden. One: the roses that weren't stolen are languishing in dank spots in the garden. Two: better do something good with all my dead—family plants. Three: we grew pineapples when we rented—we think roses might be a more grown-up iteration of the same. (It was funny to tend a plant that mirrored our personalities—a bit spiky but able to produce something good.)

He's in Stubbies short shorts and a half-button Ringers Western work shirt. I'm in black, beachy overalls which, when I asked a friend whether I should buy them, she suggested they were "a bold choice." We have a ute-load of woodchip and a cube of fresh dirt. My partner starts work on the new garden bed by digging up bits of turf and hurling them into a wheelbarrow. We'll move them to bare patches of earth later.

I take my shovel and go to my favourite rose. It hasn't been that long since I planted it in the first place. How hard could it be to transplant? The ground is cement. I lean as hard as I can on the shovel, but it barely scrapes the soil. *I should go back to the gym.* I do my best to dig out the sad rose. I'd hoped that a thick root ball would have formed, so I could take a solid lump from point a to point b. No such luck.

I put my thumb and forefinger around a lead stalk, between the thorns, and try to delicately extricate the rose and its spindly roots from the shallow hole I've scratched around it. It's stubborn. If it were a thornless shrub, I'd make a fist around the trunk and rip the sod-of-a-thing out of the ground. But it's not. It's angry, and I don't want unnecessary holes in me. On my haunches, I pull it upwards gingerly. Even though I'm trying to be gentle, when it does come away from the ground, I fall on my backside. From my bum, I take stock of the plant

I have a precarious grasp on. Its roots look even thinner and stragglier close up. *Shit.* Perhaps it would have been better to leave it in the dank spot. I'm not sure it will survive the move.

If I'm going to keep these roses alive, I should swot up. Online, I consult the green thumb oracle: *Gardening Australia*. They'll know what to do, surely.

I find a promising segment about looking after roses that aired over a decade ago in July 2010, in series 21—a time when my interest in the show waned. This episode is from the interregnum period between the two hosts I trust: the gardening guru of my childhood, Peter Cundall (the chap I watched on tele with my dad); and Costa, the affable mononymic gnome I've become familiar with in adulthood. I wonder if the advice in this old episode still holds water.

Presenter Sophie Thomson stares straight at me through the camera lens and says, "Ok, let's set the record straight. Roses are not demanding plants..."

The remainder of the segment is then dedicated to the ways in which you must fuss about meeting the rose's petty and painful demands. Nothing is as easy as they say it is. I can accept that Sophie has told me fibs to make watchable television. Would the show have stayed on the air for decades had their presenters faced the camera and said, "Ok, let's be honest. Roses are a pain in the backside?" I also know that most projects take twice as long as you expect they will. At least, I can appreciate both these ideas intellectually. Like Sophie says to close out her segment: 'It's not rocket science, is it?'

I struggle with whether that grating Australian idiom "she'll be right" applies to me. Often, I sense I am a particularly demanding plant.

I plant my favourite rose in its designated spot in the new rose garden. We push on. I put the rest of the roses in the arrangement we think will be most aesthetically pleasing. I place the block-coloured roses on either side of the rose we're growing as a standard on a special metal support frame. I move the two-tone variegated plants to the outer flanks of the single-colour bushes. I plant climbing roses to creep up the giant half-moon frame we received as chattel when we bought the place.

The next afternoon, we take a walk around the yard. We stop at the rose garden to appraise our work. The leaves on my favourite rose are wilting. Soon, if left unattended, they'll brown-off and fall on the ground. Then the whole thing will drop dead. I want to cry. I've messed up. Even though this wasn't a dead-family rose, the voice in my head berates me. *You can't even grieve right.*

"Did you pack it in properly?" my partner asks.

Probably not. It was already a delicate, sketchy operation and I didn't want to draw blood by getting too close.

"See what you reckon," I say.

He gets on his knees and sticks his finger into the dirt. "No," he says. "Not really."

He asks for potting mix, and I tell him all we have left is the expensive seed-raising mix. I've burned through bags of regular mix while potting up hydrangea cuttings.

"That'll do," he says, and marches off to collect the mix. He empties the last of the bag onto the rose. I wince. It's like he's sprinkling gold dust and saffron threads on the ground. He stomps around his scatterings and declares, "That'll do the job."

I hope so.

Days go by and I stop to check on the rose. It's thinking about living: little nodes are producing promising shades of green. But it's not happening quickly.

The ladies in my team at work love a good weather-chat on Teams. I suppose it's almost a universal constant: weather as small talk. But, in a time when most of us work from home for the bulk of the week, it offers a pleasant sense of connectedness. I'd dislike the chitchat if I didn't genuinely enjoy my colleagues' company. The banter starts at the barest hint of moisture in the air.

It's raining for all of us across Brisbane, Samford Valley, and the Sunshine Coast this afternoon, so I get useful insights from the ladies to help me on my way home from the office. They send me screenshots from "the BOM," as if I can't find this information myself.

It's true, I can't.

They're always posting snips from deep within the labyrinthine government site. *Where is the map that tells you which direction the storm is travelling?* Blows me.

My Monday office buddy, the most junior member of our team, asks if it's raining. I take any opportunity to step away from my screens and relieve my eyes, so I stroll to the window without hesitation. I can hear the rain on the roof. I milk the opportunity to relax and listen. She follows me. I feel like a terrible influence.

"It's pretty gloomy," she says from over my shoulder.

I trudge back to the computer and share what she and I have found: "Brendale office, some gloom." The day ends, and I leave work for the train station to collect my partner. It is still bleak.

When we arrive home, our little white dog is sopping. She's spent the day frolicking in the wet. A mop with stumpy legs. She bounds towards the gate to greet me.

"Hello, Annabel," I say. "You'll wiggle your tail clean off if you're not careful."

Our other fur baby lounges under my partner's car. In the wet, our blue Staffy looks like a seal. The sheen of moisture on her coat makes it spike up.

"Hello, Stevie Jean." I pat her fur back down. She's only a touch damp. Her coat seems to defy even the heaviest downpours.

I wonder how the new rose garden fared in the rain. My boots squelch in the wet grass and the sound makes me squirm. The wet patch is expanding in the leather over my toes. *My goodness.* The roses look lovely! They're green and growing.

My knees crack as I squat down to assess my favourite. It's fine. Thank god. Not only is it fine, it's happy and sprouting fresh shoots. I barely contain myself from becoming Henry Frankenstein. I want to toss my head back to the sky, stretch my arms out wide and screech, "It's alive!"

It's going to be okay. So am I.

Steph Maker is a writer and editor based on the Sunshine Coast. She currently works with an educational publisher and has a background in journalism and training. Steph loves spending time with her family, friends, and dogs. She also enjoys crafts, gardening, and leisurely breakfasts.

Victoria Street

DANI RINGROSE

The original paint is still there, but it has flaked off the walls of the house, and I am terrified that if the current owners repaint it they will erase my father and the paint cans I handed to him.

If I sneak down the driveway, my parents will not have even left the premises, because even if the house falls their initials remain etched in the carport concrete, dated 1986, and it would be clear for me to read today as an inscription on a Roman grave.

I am standing outside the house, like a trespasser. It is a worker's cottage in West End, Brisbane, a house typical of the suburb. I never knew how old it was, but let's pretend it was a turn of the century build. My parents came across it in the early 1960s, their first marital home, and left it at the beginning of the property boom in 2000. During their custodianship they had enclosed the small veranda—there are at least 100 houses in the suburb with an identical pattern that is reminiscent of the *Playschool* arched window—and repurposed the Victorian wrought iron design to be part of the fence. The hallway of the cottage was gutted like a Halloween pumpkin, creating an open plan space that modern designers would've taken notes from if they could. My parents showed me the original floor plan once, when they ripped up old carpet, the ghostly outlines of old walls appearing on the timber floorboards. It was a dark house, they said, and I could picture the shadows, the grey unpainted woods that my parents banished from the place.

Someone else has had this house for the twenty years since I have lived there, and I feel like I could step into it today and still find my parents there, unaged, my dad still alive. The house is in disrepair—a ramble—and every paint flake, every rusty drainpipe, every uneven rust-coloured paver, all have my parents' fingerprints on them. The side—it's a corner block—has an overgrown bougainvillea curling down the cyclone fence, with a sure, thick trunk that does not conjure up the twiggy mess that Dad planted just before they sold. Above the hot pink vine are two bedroom windows, one of which was mine. What would I see if I peered in the barred windows today? Surely there wouldn't be another only child, preoccupied with her world of books in a hot pink room like the inside of a fairy floss machine.

Did we repaint the hot pink before we moved? I can't remember.

Or maybe there's a surly teenager, hair dyed black, pretending to be cool and playing acoustic guitar while wrapped in an era-appropriate flannelette shirt. She holed herself up in that room an awful lot.

How would you enter the house? As I stand here now, the front door is open, security door closed across the opening. If I opened the front gate, I could guarantee, based on its crumbling state, that its hinges would carry out the same singsong melody announcing a visitor.

But there's the catch. The sound of the front gate being opened announced a stranger; the trick was to know there was a side gate behind the carport, which all friends knew to go to instead. So which gate do I open? Am I a stranger to this house now? I never used the front door; why would I start now?

I stay outside and lurk further.

They now have chickens in their backyard, as free range as our bantams were caged, but they still scratch the same dirt. It's only now that I want to join the modern movement for feathery backyard poultry that I realise how ahead of their era my parents were.

The enclosed veranda was home for our budgies, and later, where I wrote my way through essays in university. It was where I got my knee stuck between the bars of the security door as a toddler several times—turns out I am not a quick kinaesthetic learner—and wailed to wide-eyed pedestrians until Mum fetched the butter to free me. The front steps hold the echoes of my friend and I dancing the moves to *Y.M.C.A* for the neighbours to learn as we blasted it from our hi-fi system; they hold the melted drops of ice cream from evening Hava Hearts (Dad's favourite), and the condensation from the bottom of a

Strongbow Cider bottle that Mum let me try while in my younger years of high school.

I'm not sure if I'd go up the stairs barefoot though. Prior to repainting the stairs, Dad sprinkled a layer of sand on each step to stop them being so slippery. I remember tender feet when I went to check the mailbox without thongs. But would the gritty layer still be there after decades of wear?

Perhaps it's safer to go round the back. It's easy to see from the side street, but impenetrable at the same time: an urban jungle of banana trees, dusty paths between them scratched by the chickens. At times, this backyard has had an above ground pool, a rock wall, a sand pit that was scarred by streets designed for model cars, and a full-size aviary for Dad's breeding finches. Later, after we had to get rid of the bantams due to neighbour complaints, there was a mild attempt to turn the aviary into a club house, but dirt-averse, pint-sized me couldn't abide by the mulched chicken poo and it was abandoned and dismantled soon after. I remember a weirdo kid who used to zoom around like she was in a race with, of all things, the washing trolley cart. That same kid perfected her netball shots with a rusty hoop her parents installed, but she was otherwise uncoordinated and could never prove herself to the school team. Wing Defence was her default position, the one bestowed by coaches on the meekest of players.

Through the overgrown trees I can see the pavers, clay-red once, a faded pink now. My tailbone recalls the time I thought I'd use the steps to jump off while shooting netball hoops, and my legs gave me incontrovertible evidence that my brain and limbs don't often speak swiftly to each other, and the base of my spine was the first object to meet the pavers. The only time this unadventurous child ever went to the emergency ward, she scared everyone into thinking she was paralysed from the waist down. It was just bruising.

Those stairs though. Why did my parents never put railings on them? They are tall, eleven in all, reaching a doorway at least three metres off the ground that gazes at the Brisbane western storms. The current owners haven't put in railings either. Does this mean they don't have children, or just a cavalier approach to children's safety like my parents? The bottom step was a lump of rock, or maybe several rocks or bricks together, I can't remember, and I can't see through the trees now.

At the top step magpies would often gather for a feed. They would hop up the steps and warble once they reached the top to let us know they were there. Generations of baby magpies were brought up those steps, screeching and squawking. Have their grandchildren's grandchildren remained?

The back step was where Dad honed the core of our relationship together: a love of birds and a keen-eyed watcher of rumbly thunderstorms, where we'd stand at that top step and marvel as our backyard transformed to a sickly pea-soup-green under the thunderclouds. It is no coincidence that the house I will return to today, a fifteen-minute drive from here, faces west for the anticipation of those same Brisbane storms, with a vantage point three metres off the ground. This house, too, has eleven steps to a front deck, and a railing only on one side. I had never counted them before today.

No magpies feed at my current home, although one walked into our kitchen just after we bought it to give us its blessing.

Just around the edge of the back door is the bathroom, and, to inadvertently heighten my love of storms, Dad pulled out the ceiling of this room. With nothing to insulate the sound of the hammering rain on the rusted corrugated iron roof, it would make a glorious accompaniment to sitting on that top back step. Once the storms have passed on by, you could probably still rush to the front room and see them marching towards the city skyline. But when you go to sleep, you are unlikely to be accompanied by the sound of swishing tyres through rain puddles on the street outside due to all the traffic-calming speed humps.

On the other side of the house opposite, the bathroom is the kitchen, and, judging by the state of the outside, I suspect the kitchen remains a 1950s museum piece, all baby blue cupboards and exquisite joinery, not a soft-close drawer in sight. It was here that six-year-old me realised one night that I hadn't seen our dog all afternoon, and I learned that he had "gone to sleep" next to my slippery dip in the backyard. It was in the kitchen that I would share with Mum the excitement of new knowledge absorbed during my university studies. It was here that I would make myself absent from chores as an adolescent. It was here that I helped Mum assemble great bubbling lasagnes and where, one night, on a long-distance phone call from New York I demanded the recipe only to learn that it came from the back of the San Remo pasta box.

If I enter the house the illusion shatters the moment I try to grasp for the ghost of my parents. The house becomes a neglected shell and I am overwhelmed with anger at the owners for not taking good care of my parents' things. At the same time, I am achingly thankful they have not erased their trace.

So I don't.

There is a sign out the front today that says please shut the gate. This is not my house anymore, nor my parents. I have lived just as long out of the house now as I did for my first twenty years of my life.

This is no longer my neighbourhood, either. My West End of the 1980s was a mixed neighbourhood of family-owned Vietnamese restaurants and stalwart Greek families with front gardens of concrete lawns and laundry tubs overflowing with vegetable vines. Our Greek neighbours used to bake us sweet biscuits, and now, whenever I eat a melomakarona or kourambiethes, I am transported to being 5 again. We knew when our Vietnamese neighbours' son was home because when he reversed his Celica it would play a song. I can still hum it.

It's easy for me to sit up high on my pedestal declaring that the West End of the 80s and 90s was more authentic and to scoff at the "newcomers" trying to save the culture of the suburb. I remember smirking to myself the first time I saw the current owners with the "Save West End" placard on the front fence, as though I knew they weren't authentically Westenders. Yet I'm sure the traditional owners of the land of Kurilpa would scoff at my naive idea that somehow a suburb 30 years ago is more authentic than before Europeans came and erected places like Boundary Street.

But the West End of the present is still a joy. I am here today because of the Davies Park Markets. Where were our beautiful vibrant markets in the 80s and 90s? The Vietnamese bread shop we used to buy our fresh bread for breakfast on Christmas Day is still open on Vulture Street, but now there's one of the best coffee roasters in Blackstar just around the corner. The Boundary Hotel's main bar is still as seedy as ever, but the drive-through that Dad used to buy his carton of XXXX tallies from has been converted into a garden bar. The halfway houses on Russell Street are still there and the Food For Less I used to work at for 5 years was converted into—holy of holies—a shopping centre with air conditioning. I fainted three times while working because of the heat. I did so many walks along the river with my best friend in the afternoons after school, harassing the State High rowers, but it's nicer now. The industrial factories are slowly being converted into more appealing residential zoning.

I ache to touch the house. It is hard to see my parents' blood and sweat peeling away and rusting, but if the current owners tore down the vines and painted away Dad's horrible choice of gold trim, they'd be clearing away fragments of their lives. Tim Winton was right when he made *Cloudstreet* a living, breathing, personified house: my old house breathed my parents back to me so effortlessly that it made my lungs overfill and my throat catch.

Dani Ringrose (she/her) is an emerging author from Brisbane/Meanjin. She has taught high school Literature for over 20 years, and is currently studying her Masters of Writing, Editing and Publishing at UQ. For the previous 20 years, she lived in West End/Kurilpa, the setting of her piece. Find more at daniringrose.com.

Nesting Sands

ELLEN SANDERSON

"And, where are you from?"

I left my first waters reluctantly. Pushed along by Pitocin and eventually cut out of my mother's body and into my own. My first fluid free breath was taken in Geraldton, because my parents' hometown Exmouth was too small and remote to risk the odds of birth—a gamble I would have lost. Six weeks from her due date, my mother boarded a propeller plane and circled the Ningaloo reef like an uncomfortable airsick hawk before following the division of land and sea eight hours south to await my arrival. And so, I can't answer the question where are you from? Any attempt leads to either a monologue or a lie.

I've never understood where or when my body began, in air or water, or in another body entirely. If I am just a momentary vessel for an extended line of lives, do I have a singular origin? No one who lived in Exmouth really came from there. It was a transitional town where tourists came to surf and swim, and young, bikini-clad people proudly displayed enviable abdominals and prominent tan lines. It was poised on the college-ruled red line of the country's western margin—jutting out so far into the Indian Ocean that the sun both rose and set over the water. We lived as far from the geographic and ideological centre of the country's eastern states as possible, yet operated from the same Western ideas of seasonality. We ignored the intricacy of the place for time sheets and public holidays.

I grew up on a corner block, 50 meters from a hospital I wasn't born in, in a house painted a cream colour my parents insisted was light green. It hung between two verandas, red dust rising through the floorboards which the sun would catch in the late afternoon light, allowing for the illusion that time, like breath, could be held. I was out of touch—an othered observer to the slow preservation of a place that refused to evolve.

Our house blended almost seamlessly into the hot streets that smelled of sprinklers hitting dry bitumen and yellowed grass. Two white cars, two shabby boats, and a shed in Pale Eucalypt, completing the street's Colour Bond catalogue.

The town perpetually committed to the misapprehension that it was an ordinary Australian suburb. The annual flood and ebb of tourist season was paid less attention than the tides. Even the abandoned American Army base from the 1960s with its drained pool and silent bowling alley stood in inevitable stillness. The caravans crawled into town each year and spilled from the caravan park onto the crisp yellowed cricket pitch. The owners of these mobile homes erected their awnings and laid tarps to try and keep the dust at bay—a losing battle—before eventually conceding defeat and trailing out again like ants fleeing a flooded nest. People came and left. Never mind why. But I was chasing my inexorable yet distant exit. The constant tension of coming and going, staying and leaving, held me upright. I swam, sunbathed and mocked tourists knowing I was just like them, playing at ignorance like a competitive sport, pretending I wasn't unwelcome.

Resistance is an active process of suppression and redirection. Instead of moving south when the heat reached the high 40s, a three-trailer road train drove 800km, three times a day, to collect enough gas to power our air-conditioned illusion of permanence. The energy of the town rose and fell not with the place, but frequently against it. It orientated itself around Friday night footy, monthly motocross meets, and the annual GAMEX competition. Each year, 60 boats filled with 250 anglers took to the water, the florescent blue green lenses of their speed dealer sunglasses catching the sun. The competition united locals and tourists by the desire to kill the biggest fish, have their name immortalised in weekly papers, and return to the comfort of their recliners. There were big fish to be caught, dwelling deep in the open ocean and taking years to mature. The anglers set out like pageant mums from the Deep South, armed with expandable boxes of every glittering accessory imaginable. The lures were shockingly beautiful, like prawns in gymnastics costumes. Covered in fabric woven from iridescent threads that caught the light, they shimmered resplendent through the water. Society generally denies men the opportunity to accessorise unless their accessories can be justified under pragmatism. So, they smuggle their desire to be seen into flamingo office socks and cycle the streets in brilliant spandex unitards. The men of Exmouth collect sequined fishing lures and luminous green fishing line as ornaments of their manhood.

It was a chase that took hours or days, a length of time that grew with each retelling—the drama of the catch, conditions, supplies and crew always reported on in excruciating detail. If their anecdotes were to be believed, they'd hook a fish, ripping it through the weight of the water, while rescuing an esky with one hand, fighting a hammerhead with the other, and downing a stubby through a funnel. Any fight was futile; the exhaustion became suffocating. The fish didn't get a chance at "humane slaughter". They died before they hit the deck. This is not something you realise when the carcass of a 10-year-old marlin appears on your Tinder feed, displayed proudly in the arm of its grinning predator—no, Dave, I don't want to see your tackle.

The winning fish was displayed in ice-delayed decay, staring out of dead eyes on newspapers and TV screens. It was discussed at the petrol station, and in line at the IGA. Whether you participated in the competition or not, your waking hours became consumed by this notable death. The time, weight, size, and cost of the kill were recited, proof that the victor had conquered the town, the competitors, and the sea itself. He (normally he) could measure his belonging in any metric asked of him.

I had no metrics. Girlhood barred my access. While he stood grinning, thrilled with the weight of his catch, gut swollen from beer and bad habits, I knew I would not be given the privilege of being weighed by my achievement. My worth would be, and already was, determined by my physical weight, by the space I couldn't help but take up. At school, I wasn't a good girl; they were petite and quiet, never finished lunch. I tried to emulate them, but I couldn't do it. I was always ravenous, host to a hunger that could not be contained. I did not want a belonging that was conditional. I could not prove my worth or connection to the place, and eventually I persuaded myself into believing I had none.

The town rallied for the competition; the stage set perfectly for the performance of hegemonic masculinity. Fishing, sport (watching or playing), surfing, playing in a band, drinking: the activity itself matters very little if it is something that can be won. Women don't need an activity; under the patriarchy, whoever is thinnest wins. The competitive urge to shrink ourselves is ever present. It wasn't that women didn't have a place in Exmouth; the biggest event of the season was when the whales brought their calves.

There she is to the left, everybody; she's got her baby with her, and she's brought him all the way up here for the warm water, to feed him up. The wind-chilled onlookers murmured their approval of her fine mammalian mothering as if she was deeply deserving of their endorsement. Yes, we've seen a whale... how big she was... and how lucky we are, because you never know what you'll get on the day. They had to trivialise her pursuit, or sit with the discomfort that they would never know the depths of her. She made a ripple in the surface of their lives just strong enough to carry them home.

Women were rooted into the place and the town, they were essential but in a way I couldn't emulate or understand. My mother was a natural, she lived community first. She married my Dad on a local beach at the end of turtle nesting season in a cream dress and no shoes. For their anniversary, we returned to that beach huddled over cheese sandwiches and roughly chopped fruit salad, awaiting the arrival of an expectant mother. The loggerhead turtle moved so slowly that any excitement I felt at her tentative emergence from the shallows had elapsed by the time she reached the dry sand. She was visibly uncomfortable even in the evening light. Her yellow-brown flippers, host to a film of algae, curved perfectly to propel her through the water, not to hoist her through the sand. Each movement an exhaustive effort to heave a body, rendered cumbersome by the temperamental ridges of the shore. She seemed resigned to the process; her flippers had trudged along that beach many times before. As a loggerhead, she was able to navigate back to her hatching place with astonishing accuracy to lay her own clutch.

I wondered if she remembered her own hatching, emerging from the fine strength of her shell to the fragments of sand, the way it slipped below her flippers as she sank unsteadily. Could she remember that first pull to the sea? Or was she like me, with no memory of a time without the ocean? I assumed so. Eventually, when the light grew bored of her measured pace and she decided she was close enough to the dunes, she began to dig. The rhythmic scrape of shifting sands syncopated with the waves' steady exhale onto the beach. I sat among the dunes and breathed with the place. When the percussive sound ceased, I directed the orange beam of my torch towards the nest. An egg, rendered momentarily pellucid by the torchlight, pushed from her body, fell softly onto the prepared sands below. The beach was a place of motherhood and of girlhood; a place women made their own by returning to struggle year after year. Knowing the risk and accepting the discomfort of survival.

As I sat in her absence, my mother's worn polo fleece jumper wrapped around my body, I wondered what it would look like for one of her ovoid daughters to reject that lineage of maternity. I was a very expensive and much anticipated IVF baby, the only continuation of the Bates (my maternal grandmother's) line, making my mother the first woman in her family to actively pursue motherhood. The women that came before her did not so much choose motherhood as inherit it.

As far as I know, none of the girls I grew up with hated Exmouth like I did. Especially not B, my closest friend. In my earliest memory of her, I was wading through the shallows pulling two toy tugboats on strings with the kind of sombre dedication only a three-year-old is capable of. B and her parents were walking up the beach towards us. She was determined not to hold her Dad's hand even when the bigger waves approached. I liked her immediately. She asked if she could play with my boats, and I told her they were very little, with a very important job, and that they needed a break, so she had to be gentle. Our friendship was solidified as she solemnly accepted the string. I loved those boats; I used to imagine them expanded to scale, trailing behind me, showing my strength. My obsession began after watching them escort the prawn trawlers into the marina at the end of the day. Now all I think about is the people on those trawlers working on 457 visas that everyone in town claimed was a great deal for them.

Together, B and I grew up in the shallows. My eyes fixed beyond the dunes; hers reflected the sea. We played pirates in the inlets; she boldly hunted mud crabs. I walked unsteadily, nose upturned from the foul scent of mud and mangroves, avoiding the sharp finger roots extending from the filth that feeds and raises an entire ecosystem. She was older, braver, and thinner than me. None of that has changed. Even as a child, she had the kind of ease that comes with the permission which thinness grants girls and women. It was an ease I was constantly aware I did not possess; I was unable to exist without disturbing or disrupting anyone else. B was always able to fit in the small spaces, between others in the back of cars, on laps and into the clothes I had outgrown. Her frame carried clothes perfectly, giving her the opportunity to express who she was or wasn't without her body interfering with the message as mine always did. This smallness gave her permission to be present, it made her nice, it allowed her to join the group and ask nothing of them.

The only moments of conformity I could manage were found in time spent with Dad. Our father-daughter days often involved squidding and always included peanut butter sandwiches. Once we'd launched the dinghy, attached the glittering lures, and positioned the rods, and let the line out for a few seconds we powered loudly through the waves. As he sat at the back of the dinghy beside the rudder, I positioned myself on the bow, flat on my stomach, life jacket cushioning the impact of the tin as we bounced along the ridges of the water. The wind and speed made hats pointless, giving way to the sun beaming off the water, searing my skin and turning my ears pink.

The boat would slow as if cut from an invisible line drawing it forward, and I swivelled to see Dad reaching for a rod with a line drawn taut. A squid had fallen for our pantomime prawn. Its skin, semi-transparent and dazzling with speckles, formed concentric circles of coruscating colours—a dance of aged oranges, soft purples and incandescent greens choreographed just for us. I was so taken in by the display I never stopped to notice my cruelty in the dry eyes of the creature. I would peer down at it, terrified and fascinated by its unpredictability and wonder how alike we might be. Was I capable of such aggressive self- expression? Would I have to wait for my death to attempt it? Was it a girl like me?

It's very difficult to determine the biological sex of a living squid or cuttlefish. The only way is to place them in front of a mirror and observe their reaction. Males react aggressively to other males, including their own reflections, and display a striped pattern revealing their sex. I pity a sexed squid, free and self-determined until you force it to fight the self in the mirror. Squid take their rage and fear and transform it into miraculous colours and shapes unique to the predator or prey they face. They morph their sensitive, fleshy frills from one form to the next, never allowing who they appear to be to affect who they will become. As it flapped and flashed its brilliant dying colours, the squid in the bucket readied itself for its ultimate act of diffusion, dissolving into a pool of its own ink. A momentary illusion of limitlessness, there and not there, bodied and boundless.

I left my nesting sands crammed awkwardly into the wing seat of a loud propeller plane. As it rose, I watched the lines dividing the blue, white and red of the environment dissipate, the boarders bleeding into each other. I can no more draw lines around myself than around that landscape, and I have no interest in defining either.

Ellen grew up in a remote coastal town without bookstores but surrounded by the sea. She enjoys reading, reflecting on, and writing about messy, paradoxical emotions. In her writing, Ellen draws on her coastal upbringing by exploring the interaction between human nature and the natural world.

Names Have Been Changed

MARINA DELLER

This is a work of non-fiction. Names have been changed as an act of protection. Names have been changed because the weight of the letters was too heavy to bear.

My father was mad when I lopped his name off the end of mine. He felt I was erasing him. I guess in a way I was trying to.

I decided I didn't want to wear his name anymore the day after he changed the locks. My barely sixteen-year-old brother had to sleep on a park bench because he couldn't get into his—*our*—home. My brother, my sister, and I were teenagers treading grief's waters after our mum's death. Our dad's own waves of loss washed over us, threatening to drown us. Though afflicted by the loss of the same dear person, we were afflicted in entirely different ways. He left, unexpectedly, for weeks at a time. If we were lucky, he'd call and we'd get a few words mumbled down a staticky line, an unfamiliar woman's voice in the background. We could hear the woman laughing. When we told our dad we missed him, were struggling without him, his response was to shut us out both emotionally and literally.

The moment he changed the locks, my father became someone I didn't recognise. I imagined cutting his name off with scissors, leaving only my dead mother's name and a hyphen—hanging. Locks, lops, scissors, keys. It makes sense to me. I heard somewhere that when you cut off a leg, it's best to cut below the knee. The hyphen was a reminder, a signal, that something was once there. I snipped it too and was left with Mum's last name only.

Grief and loss bred grief and loss until it was all we were made of.

In the end, I felt I was cutting the name of a stranger.

Mum had a fraught relationship with names. Her dad used to spell her name differently; her initials were KJ, but he called her CJ. I'm not sure if he was trying to piss off his estranged ex-wife, my grandmother, or lay some kind of individualised, personalised claim to Mum. I don't know what the story was. I just know it made Mum feel odd, fractured. If she couldn't trust her own initials, what could she trust?

In some way, I know how she felt. Parents are the ones who teach us reality; they tell us how to see the world and what to believe. And then, later, when we unlearn some of it, or learn *more* of it, we look back at them with new eyes. Although I cannot ask her, I know this is an experience my mum and I must have shared. We reexamined our beloved fathers in young adulthood and found behaviours we didn't admire. We found the information they gave us, the names they gave us, wanting.

Mum was married three times and gained a new last name each time. But she always attached the new names with a hyphen—tacked them on after *her* last name. My older half-siblings have names which half-match mine. We share the same first last-name, the name that I kept. It tethers us to one another, to her, like strands of thread.

My friend tells me she wants to change her last name too. Hers is also attached to a father she couldn't be farther from. Farther still than I am from mine, and without the excuse of grief's grip. Her father is unforgivably shit. Though my friend's last name is short, the letters are heavy.

She considers changing it to her partner's name, but his is also inherited from an absent father. All those goddamn absent fathers. All those goddamn names. After getting engaged they consider their options: combine the two names or reach for something completely new?

"I love the idea of choosing something new," I say. "Cheryl Strayed did that." A memoirist and advice columnist, Cheryl Strayed also wrote about losing herself after losing her mum.

All those dead mothers.

"If I were to choose a name," I tell my friend, "I think I'd also choose a verb. Something which implies movement, *doing*."

It is six years post-lock change, in one of the rare months where Dad and I orbit one another, full of paradoxically cautious hope for a repaired relationship. At his house, the house which was once ours, he walks me through his small garden. He points out gently curling vines, diminutive yet fragrant potted fruit trees, ripening tomatoes. Through the windows, I can see he has turned my bedroom into a study. We drink coffee at the dining table I've eaten more meals at than any other in my life, then make our way to the garage. He is sorting through the few items he didn't discard immediately after Mum's death. This includes one of Mum's old sketch books. He hands it to me, along with a yellowing ID card from her early days at university, and an envelope with a lock of my own hair within. I'm writing my thesis about objects of grief. He knows this. I think he's trying to help.

Back in the safety of my dingy sharehouse, I flick through the sketchbook pages that are filled with slanted lead lines. Mum has sketched oranges on a table in shadow. There is a moon out of the window. There are people I do not know with expressions I cannot place. In every margin, Mum's looping handwriting hints at the scenes. "Shearing shed," "stained glass." The words "Iris" and "Moon" are always together. *Iris Moon*. I realise that her younger self was signing a new name for herself. An artist's name? Something entirely hers? I think this is the truth, but I will never know. Can it be true if I—we—will never know for sure?

We used to play a game in the car when we were bored—what is the root of this word? Dad studied Latin and delighted in telling us where each of our favourite phrases originated. Marina, my first name, translates to *from the sea*. This is quite a romantic notion, but I usually introduce myself with a far more practical comparison: "It's 'Marina' like the place you put boats."

When I was younger, I thought I was secretly a mermaid. A beloved Shirley Barber book with a mermaid named Marina is the culprit of that misconception. In reality, my parents named me for a character in a lesser-known (debatably) Shakespearian play called *Pericles, Prince of Tyre*. My parents were both English lecturers, both poets. Mum already had two children when she met my dad; he had one. Mums' kids had Shakespearian names too.

Play-Marina is a virtuous young lady kidnapped by pirates, who want to force her into sex work. They quickly realise, however, that she is far too pure to be thrust into the profession and thus they hire her out as a music teacher. Mum's desire to continue naming her children after Shakespearian characters must have won over questionable plot points.

It is one of the months where we decidedly do *not* orbit one another, where the cracks of loss have opened into a yawning chasm between us. One of my siblings tells me that Dad is mad I don't use his name. Dad saw that I had changed it on social media and had published creative work without it stamped in the byline. I think it is this second one which hurt him the most.

I often feel that as the child of a writer my successes belong to him, are his to claim, but my failures are all my own. I have not plucked this feeling from thin air, I read it between his praise and put downs in the years following Mum's death. *Brilliant! Liar. Lovely. Useless! Bright. Child.*

Although at the time removing his name felt like a decision born of death, perhaps it was also one born of life—a new creative life I aimed to forge for myself.

This feels true, I am my own person.

But, I am also still their child. I cannot change this. I wouldn't want to, even in their absence.

Another friend of mine decides to change their name. In this case, their first name. They search for something which fits them better, which reflects their true gender and true self. At first, they drop the letters behind their initial—snip, snip, snip, snip. Two vowels, two constants, gone. A solitary letter remaining. This works for a while, but it's a stepping stone of sorts. A path to follow, a thread to weave. Eventually they cut the last letter and fashion a completely new name for themselves instead. In doing so, they *become* themselves.

"Us queers are more aware of the power of names than most," they say. We're sitting on a park bench eating vanilla slice. I move my hands in a flurry of agreement and shreds of coconut fall like snow from the pastry.

"Yes!" I say. "We are aware of how we wear them—for better or worse. Labels can be a comfort. They can be a curse."

"And names sometimes even more than other labels. A name is like home," my friend says.

"Funny," I say, "I've just been thinking the same thing."

The power of writing means I can give myself any name I like. I can slip names on and off. Mostly, it feels odd, tricky, like trying to shimmy out of wet bathers. The names resist against my skin, gather where they should glide. I know it is not the case for all queers, or indeed many queers, but nothing *sounds* quite as right as the name my parents gave me. Nothing fits me quite as well.

"Marina?" the Uber driver asks.

"Yep," I nod as I duck into the back seat of his car.

"I have never met such a young Marina, only old women."

"I hear that a lot. I've only ever met Marinas who are older than me too."

"Oh, yes? Why is your name Marina? I'm Italian. You're not Italian. So blonde, so many freckles!"

He's right, I'm not Italian. It's usually one of the first things people ask, as well as singing a song, previously unfamiliar to me, where many of the lyrics are a melodic chanting of *"Marina, Marina, Marina..."*

"Marina, Marina, Marina..." the Uber driver croons. "Do you like your name?"

I consider the question. I haven't been asked this before. While I might chop away at my last name, and try on names like hats when I write, my first name is a golden coin heavy and safe in my pocket. My parents weighed the letters, measured them, brought them home, to a house with striped green bedsheets and a lemon tree in the yard, a house full of love. That version of them, of me, is the one I want to hold close, even as I forge new futures.

"Yes," I tell the driver. "I like it."

My name is the beginning of a story I am only just learning how to tell.

Marina Deller is a writer, critic, and creative with a PhD in Creative Writing from Flinders University of South Australia. They tell stories of identity, bodies, and grief in outlets such as Voiceworks, Archer, Baby Teeth Journal, and Westerly.

(22) Versions of 15

EMILY O'DWYER

21. Little Birdy says it more articulately: "my brother taught me how to fly," to soar out of misery. Knowing what I know now, he was mad at the world too. We were both depressed, trying to clutch onto joy.
18. Ali gave me back my body, so I could just be in the car with my brother.
12. "Why are you getting so angry?" my dad would ask.
22. Because nothing sparks a light of energy more than rage. It shows me I have a little fight left. It's glorious. It's what women are made of.
13. "Give us a smile. Act like a real lady," Ali calls out the statements that incite my rage.
1. Was 15 sweet? I think I was sweet. I can hear my dad laughing at this in my head. Not so much.
10. Something perfectly ripe for comments and stares from older, and old men. To paraphrase another of my favourite singers: I wasn't that old, but I was too old for that shit.
0. "Such a sweet age", my classmate said when she remembered back to her first boyfriend.
4. Was it really that transparent though, my rage towards the world?
8. My brother is emotional, caring, loving but he was drowning because these traits were pushed to the back of his mind as weaknesses, until the only acceptable emotion he was left with was rage. Towards the world, fairly, and towards me, unfairly.
11. Because 15 is sweet. Too sweet to be talked about in a way that makes your body not yours anymore.
14. I could never answer my dad's question, articulately. But I felt it. I

found it in Ali's words.

20. It's the most complicated love, to always have a person who can drive you to the deepest foundations of your fury, but also be your protector and safe place.

19. When I think of him, I think of joy, drenched in sadness, swirling around love and hate and rage.

2. I remember two words: girlie bits. A song by Ali Barter. I remember my brother driving us home. I was ready for an argument.

"You'll love this one, Em," he played the song, my feminist awakening.

5. He was growing up in a world telling him that to be a man was to make fun of those who are weak, to speak crudely about girls who showed too much skin, to call 14-year-olds out for looking like sluts.

3. Sweet. Just for a moment. How nice is it when someone sees you, and they just let you be.

7. He was taught it was up to him to decide.

6. In whose eyes?

9. I was learning that my body was an object to be gawked at. Not a child, not a woman. But not too young, not too innocent anymore.

15. My brother recognised it. There was no need to explain anything to each other.

16. I had to really think about this moment to realise this was sweet, but I remember it because of rage. Happiness was hiding under bigger feelings, in smaller moments.

17. "What's a woman really made of? Something glorious."

Emily O'Dwyer is a journalist and creative writer living in Brisbane. She has written articles for Women in Tourism Indonesia. O'Dwyer loves writing to express all the things she can't quite with her words (verbal that is). She is currently working on a script. Several of her articles are due to be published later this year.

About Jacaranda Journal

Headquartered at the University of Queensland, Jacaranda is a literary journal publishing standout works of short fiction, creative non-fiction, and poetry from new and emerging writers. As a volunteer-run organisation, Jacaranda's mission is to provide a supportive editorial process, as well as a stylish print and online publication through which contributors can showcase the full potential of their work to a wide audience.

The first issue of Jacaranda was published in 2013 by a determined group of students at the University of Queensland on the conviction that the best way to grow and succeed in the literary world is together. To date, fourteen editions of Jacaranda have been put to print: one each year between 2013 and 2022, and two editions in 2023 and 2024. Earlier editions published work exclusively from UQ's writing cohort, including academic essay, criticism, fiction, and poetry.

Since 2023, Jacaranda has opened up submissions to include new and emerging writers of poetry, fiction, and non-fiction from right across Australia.

About the Editors

Francis Harvey is a Brisbane-based writer and editor who commits his energy to developing the work of his peers. Following an internship at Griffith Review in 2023, he has taken on the role of Editor in Chief at Jacaranda Journal for 2024. He is concurrently completing a masters degree in Writing, Editing and Publishing at University of Queensland, where his dissertation research focuses on the impact of AI on trade publishing.

Siena Johnstone is completing her Bachelor of Arts at the University of Queensland in English Literature, Writing and Communications. Siena is deeply interested in literature and research that explores the intricacies of the human experience and how we connect and relate to each other and ourselves. In her professional life, Siena is a copywriter and content designer who has worked across Australia, North America, and the United Kingdom.

www.ingramcontent.com/pod-product-compliance
Lightning Source LLC
Chambersburg PA
CBHW010352170726
48290CB00010B/2692